Machine Major Boysie Gann had been assigned to duty far beyond Pluto, on Polaris Station, one of the artificial sun-satellites protecting the inner planets—and Earth—from the Reefs of Space.

For the Starchild had sent an ultimatum to Earth, calling on the Plan of Man to relinquish its total control over humanity under threat of frightful reprisals . . . and as proof of his powers, the Starchild had threatened to extinguish the sun and a dozen near stars for a period of time.

But Boysie didn't know anything about the Starchild. All he knew was his job—to find out who on Polaris Station was violating the Plan of Man.

He found out—and before he could do anything about it, he was captured, marooned on a Reef, and accused of being the Starchild himself!

To survive, Boysie had to find out who, or what, the Starchild might be. And all he knew for sure was that the Starchild did in fact have the power to stop the Sun if he wanted to!

All published by Ballantine Books

STARCHILD

Frederik Pohl

and

Jack Williamson

BALLANTINE BOOKS • NEW YORK

SBN 345-23449-9-125

First Printing: November, 1965
Second Printing: August, 1973

Printed in the United States of America

Cover art by Jacques Wyrs

BALLANTINE BOOKS, INC.
201 E. 50th Street, New York, N.Y. 10022

I

It was the day, the hour, and the moment of Earth's vernal equinox . . . and the near stars blinked.

A dozen of them flickered at once. Blazing Sirius and its dense dwarf sister. The bright yellow twins of Alpha Centauri. Faint red Proxima . . . the distant sparks of Eta Eridani and 70 Ophiuchi A . . . the bright Sun itself.

The vast cosmic engines declared a vacation in their processes: the fusion of smaller atoms into large, the flow of surplus mass into energy, the filtration of that energy through layered seas of restless gas, the radiation of their atomic power into space.

By the shores of Earth's oceans, within the crater walls of Luna, on the sands of Mars and the ringed satellites of Saturn, out past the Spacewall to the Reefs, the great billion-headed human race stirred and shook and knew fear. The whisper spread out into the galaxy, propagated at the speed of light: *"The Starchild!"*

That was the way it began.

The flickering of the neighbor stars lasted only a moment, and it was seen first on the Reefs nearest each star. Then slow Pluto caught the twinkle of 70 Ophiuchi A while Neptune, lumbering in its dark orbit on the far side of Sol, was the first to catch the dimming of white-hot Sirius. On Earth, where the fat old Planner sat chuckling

5

on his golden chair, every momentary pulse of darkness arrived at once. His chuckles stopped. His pouchy face darkened. As his astronomers reported in, he exploded in wrath.

His first reports came from a hardened station in the zone of twilight on the planet Mercury, where sliding concrete doors uncovered a pit beneath a saw-toothed crater rim.

A silvered dome pushed out of the pit, out of the ragged shadow, into the white blaze of the near sun. The barrels of a dozen optical and radio telescopes, pyrometers, telescanners, and cameras thrust out at the great orb, under the blazoned slogan that the dome displayed to the universe in letters of cast bronze:

THE MIGHTIEST REWARDS
THE MOST FAITHFUL

And inside the insulated, refrigerated observatory, three astronomers watched a thousand boards and gauges and dials. They were waiting.

For they had been warned.

The senior officer on duty lifted his eyes from a chronometer dial and growled, "Five minutes!"

The other two men squinted at their instruments in silence. The grizzled Technicaptain peered at them through the pale lighting of the screen that dominated the glitter of instruments. On it swam the visual image of the sun, golden and engorged, reaching out with fat, slow tendrils of superheated gas as it lay above the rock-fanged horizon of the planet Mercury.

"Yeah," he grumbled, half to himself. "We're ready."

The junior member of the team was a lean young Technicadet, an ambitious young man already embittered by the harsh facts of survival and promotion in the Technicorps. He dared a comment: "Ready for nothing, if you ask me. This is idiot business!"

The senior officer rolled a yellowed eye toward him, but said nothing.

"So?" murmured the third man. He was a plump little Techtenant who had found a satisfying philosophy in his recent promotion. "The Machine's business is idiotic, then?"

"Now, look! I didn't mean—"

"No. But you didn't think, either. The Machine discerns the greater plan; we only execute the parts. If the Machine attaches importance to this fanciful creature, the Starchild, then we may not question its motives."

The Technicadet gestured at the huge solar globe angrily and cried, "Look! What could put *that* out?"

The Techtenant shrugged, and the senior officer said only, "Four minutes."

The cadet's military courtesy was worn thin under the abrasion of their long, tense vigil. He scowled at his telemetering pyrometers and grumbled, "Not a flicker! We've been here three miserable weeks, and we haven't seen a thing."

The Technicaptain rumbled, "We'll stay here three years if the Machine orders it. The Machine is above injustice or error. The Machine was built to rule the Plan, and it is guarded against human blunders."

"Oh, yes, sir. But we've seen nothing at all," cried the Technicadet. "No Starchild. No major sunspots—or whatever it is we are supposed to expect."

"Practice patience," advised the fat captain. "Or you may find yourself serving the Plan more personally. There is always a need for spare parts in the Body Bank! Three minutes."

The Technicadet subsided grudgingly apologetic. All three men sat strapped in their observation chairs, watching the great golden image of the sun. Wreathed in its red coronal streamers, pocked in its middle latitudes with a trail of small black spots, it hung over the black horizon like a god's eye. The instruments around them clicked and murmured.

"I remember," the Techtenant said at last, as if to himself, "when that Sun was only another star in the sky. No brighter even than great Vega."

The Technicadet cried eagerly, "You were out in the Reefs?"

"Two minutes," growled the captain, but his eyes were on the young Techtenant.

He nodded. "Looking for my sister's . . . boy friend? Fiance? Looking for Boysie Gann. Because he was looking for the Starchild. And we didn't find either of them."

The cadet said simply, "I've never seen the Reefs."

"A beautiful thing," said the Techtenant. "There are spiked forests of silicon plants, shining with their own light. Like jewels, and sharp enough to shred your spacesuit. There's a growth that makes great brain-shaped masses of pure silver. There are thick stalks of platinum and gold, and there are things like flowers that are diamonds."

The cadet's breathing was suddenly loud. The grizzled old captain turned to look at him, all his recent scorn now frozen into longing—and a sort of fear. He snapped: "Pay attention to your work, man! The Reefs are dangerous business!"

"Yes, sir," the Techtenant agreed earnestly. "I saw a great beast like a nightmare, shaped like a scorpion, huge as a horse—"

"No, you fool! Dangerous to the Plan of Man. There is something there that nearly destroyed us once. If the Starchild has his way—"

He stopped himself and said only, "One minute."

The Techtenant reddened. "I'm sorry, sir. I certainly did not intend to seem unplanned. I don't mean to suggest that those savage nomads beyond the Spacewall are worth considering, even if they do believe the Starchild to be more than human."

"Tend your instruments!" The captain set the example, resolutely taking his eyes from the men and the screen, clamping them on the bank of gauges and dials before him. A vagrant thought stirred his mind of the blond Togetherness girl who had first whispered the name of the Starchild to him. What had become of her? The Body Bank?

—But there was no time for that. It was only seconds now.

In spite of all the insulation and the cold air sighing from the vents, the dome was suddenly stifling. The captain felt a trickle of perspiration running down his sides. "Twenty seconds!"

The captain stood with his eyes frozen on the black chronometer needle that raced to meet the red, still one he had set. When they touched it would be the vernal equinox on Earth. And the Starchild's threat would be proved an empty bluff . . . or would not.

Suddenly the whisper of the instruments changed. A camera shutter began clicking gently.

"Ten seconds!"

The shielded floor lamps shut themselves off. Only the instrument lights rivaled the phosphor glow from the image of the great yellow sun in the screen.

"Five seconds! . . . Four! . . . Three! . . ."

Twenty reels of tape began to spin shrilly in the darkness; the breathing of the men was like sobs.

"Two! . . . One! . . .

"Zero!"

The captain gulped and rubbed his eyes.

There was a dimming. Then the filters went down, and then there was a burst of flame—then darkness.

The lights were gone. All of them. The Sun's image

had winked out. He heard a gasp from one of the other men, then a shout. "The Starchild! He's done it!"

And the other man sobbed, "We're blind!"

That, too, was how it began. But there was more.

Like a ripple from a pebble dropped into a still pond, a wave of darkness spread out from the sun. Three minutes after the instant of the vernal equinox it reached that clucking camera in the dome on Mercury, unseen by those sightless eyes.

In not quite three more minutes, it struck the men watching from the orbital stations above the eternal hot, dank clouds of Venus. A falling shadow of fear, it darkened their screens, whitened their faces, silenced their talk. But their instrument lights remained visible. They had not been blinded by that last great burst of light from the Sun.

Eight minutes from the Sun, the wave of blackness washed over Earth. All across the sunward face of the planet a crushing night came down. Bewildered, men paused and fumbled through the endless seconds before the city lights came on. Terror electrified those who had heard the whisper of the Starchild's threat. On the dark side of Earth and on Luna, astronomers blenched as their near, familiar stars flickered. Some had heard whispers of the Starchild too, and of a Writ of Liberation. Others merely knew that the images in their great space-borne mirrors, or in the scopes that peered up from Earth's highest mountains, suddenly were missing familiar points of light.

They came back . . .

But the Sun did not. Not then. Not for half an hour and more, and while it was gone there was panic.

To the Planner on his great golden chair the news came and quenched his chuckling good humor. His huge soft face turned pale with fear.

To a man named Boysie Gann, locked in the dungeons of the Machine, no word came—but he knew. For he heard a guard whisper to another, *"The Starchild!"*

To a girl with haunted dark eyes, telling whispering sonic beads before a console of the Machine, the word came in a language that Man had not invented, and few men could understand. Her name was Delta Four, and she did not fear. She did not care at all. . . .

And that was how it began for them, and the wave of darkness raced on into infinite space.

Twelve minutes from the Sun it swept Mars, halting the dedication of an enormous new project to extract oxygen and water from the dead crust of the planet. The Deputy Planner of Mars, a poorly planned individual who had seen the Writ of Liberation with his own eyes, snatched a gun from his honor guard and shot himself.

During the following quarter hour that shadow bathed the asteroids, terrified a few, left others unconcerned. For either they did not know, being buried in the mining shafts that hollowed out the precious cores of the tiny planets, or they were so dazed and uncaring with the eternal hardship of their toil that nothing could frighten them again.

The racing wave of light overtook the scattered outposts of the Plan on the Moons of Jupiter. It darkened Saturn's rings, swallowed the satellites of Uranus and Neptune. It fell upon the Spacewall Command complex on distant Pluto, where only those whose eyes fell upon the Sun by chance noticed it—but they were afraid.

It drowned the Spacewall itself—more web than wall, a net of far-scattered stations whose laser beams and patrol craft kept watch on the little-known infinities beyond, alert to guard the Plan of Man against vagrants from the Reefs, or such enemies as the Starchild.

A wave of unexpected terror, it sent the crews of a thousand slow-wheeling spaceforts shouting to their emergency stations. It awakened sirens and horns on ten thousand lonely patrol ships. It set the laser beams winking with a million signals of confused alarm.

A day or so beyond Pluto it washed the frontiers of the solar system, the snowball protoplanets of solid methane and ammonia that the distant gravitational arms of the Sun had never gathered into actual worlds.

And then at last, days beyond that last fearful outpost of the Plan, it began to bathe the Reefs of Space.

Out on the reefs, those living asteroids grown through unending ages by the minute fusorian organisms, feeding on the thin seas of interstellar hydrogen, the wave of shadow no longer meant terror. It was only another event in a life that was filled with danger and surprise.

On one lonely worldlet a prospector stopped to peer in annoyance at where the Sun had been. He fumbled in his pack for a luminous crystal of fusorian diamond, and bent over his drill again.

On another reef a lay preacher in the Church of the Star glanced at his watch, then at the sky. He was not afraid when he saw that Sol was gone from its accustomed position. He had been expecting it.

He left his work to face the blue blaze of Deneb, knelt, whispered a few words of supplication and thanksgiving. Calmly then he bent back to the unfinished space boot on his last, for he was by trade a cobbler.

The shadow washed over a grave, but no one saw it. No one could have, for no one was there. Not even the cadaver; the grave was empty.

The shadow rested lightly on a city of stern, hardfaced refugees from the Plan of Man—on a great cluster of reeflets where a mighty space armada was being fashioned from fusorian steel—on a girl named Quarla Snow, who stood watching it flicker out with tears bright in her eyes.

On another living rock, a herdsman stood guarding a

calving member of his herd from a flight of marauding pyropods. Lying behind a sheltering ledge of organic iron, one eye on his parturient spaceling while he searched out the armored killers with frugal flashes from his laser gun, he failed to notice that the Sun had gone out.

That was how it began, for every man, woman and child alive.

And thirty-nine minutes later the Sun began again its mighty outpouring of heat and light, but the wave of brilliance that followed the dark looked down on a changed solar system.

The Sun's atomic engines ran again. Hydrogen fused into helium through the carbon cycle. Filtered energy flowed toward the solar surface. Radiation poured into space.

Three minutes from the Sun, the wave of radiation crashed against that insulated dome on Mercury. It was recorded by the clucking camera, analyzed by the thousand automatic instruments. Sobbing with joy—or fear! —the blinded astronomers flashed the word to Earth: *The Sun lives again!*

But its light reached Earth before their message.

That first rebirth of light brushed a high mountain on Earth, where the Planner sat on his golden chair, the gray metal falcon that perched on his shoulder darting a red-eyed glare about the room, whirring its steel wings. The Planner was staring at a sheet of creamy parchment that bore the heading:

WRIT OF LIBERATION

It had been delivered to him by the hand of one of his own guards, who had found it at his door. It said:

The Starchild requires the release of all of his followers who are held in the service of the Plan of Man by security collars.

The Starchild requires that all of his followers who have been consigned to the Body Bank for salvage shall be restored to their original state, and then that they too shall be released.

The Starchild finally requires that the barrier called the Spacewall shall be dismantled, and that free passage between the worlds of the Plan and the Reefs of Space shall be permitted.

The Starchild is aware that the Plan of Man considers itself invulnerable, and thus he has arranged a warning demonstration. At the moment of the vernal equinox on Earth the Sun will be extinguished. Twelve near stars will blink.

If the Planner fails to meet the Starchild's requirements after this demonstration, further measures will be taken. These will result in the destruction of the Plan of Man.

"Unplanned nonsense," groaned the Planner. "Impudence! Treason!"

A tall Technicolonel said uneasily, "Sir. We must take measures—"

"Measures," grumbled the Planner while his steel falcon clashed its pinions. "What does the Machine say?"

A girl in a hooded gown said, "No data, sir." Her voice was like distant music, her expression serene.

"No data! Find me some data! Find who this Starchild is! Tell me how he did this thing—and how I can stop him from doing it again!"

The Technicolonel coughed. "Sir, for some years we have had reports of a Church of the Star. A new religion, apparently springing from the Reefs—"

"Always the Reefs! They should have been destroyed twenty years ago!"

"Yes, sir. But they were not. And the pioneers—that is, sir, the tramps and vagabonds on the Reefs—they invented new superstitions. They worship, I believe, the star Deneb. Alpha Cygni—the star at the top of the Northern Cross. They have imagined a paradise on the planets that they imagine to orbit around it. They wish to migrate there, or some of them do—though at maximum drive for conventional spacecraft," he continued earnestly, "they might average some one per cent of the speed of light, in which case Deneb, at four hundred light-years distance, would not be reached for forty thousand—"

"Get to the point!" cried the Planner fretfully. "What about the Starchild?"

"Well, sir we had heard rumors of such a person in our investigations of this cult. Some time ago we decided to send a . . . uh . . . a special investigator to secure intelligence concerning him and it. The investigator's name was Boysie Gann, sir, and—"

"Bring him to me! Is he here on Earth?"

"Yes, sir. But . . . well, sir, he did not return as we expected. In fact"—the Colonel's face was a picture puzzle of confusion—"I *must confess,* sir, that we don't properly know how he *did* return, as—"

"Fool!" shouted the Planner. "Bring him to me! Never mind what you don't know. Bring me Boysie Gann!"

And that too was how it began; but in fact, some parts of it began earlier.

For Boysie Gann it began many months earlier, when he was a spy.

II

For Boysie Gann the beginning was on Polaris Station, that great metal wheel that floats in the icy space past Pluto, one link in the Spacewall between the Plan of Man planets and the Reefs.

Boysie Gann was twenty-six years old and already a Machine Major.

Boysie Gann was six feet tall, brown-haired, blue-eyed. He was broad through the shoulders and slim at the waist. He moved like a cheerful cat. He looked like a fighter, and he was.

He reported aboard the Polaris Station with a grin and a disarming look out of his bright blue eyes. "Boysie Gann reporting, sir," he told the deck officer. "Technicadet Gann, at your service." And that was a cheerful lie. He was no cadet, but at the spy school on Pluto the briefing officers had given him a new rank to make his job easier. A Machine Major was a man of importance. He would be watched. A cadet could go anywhere, see anything.

The deck officer assigned him quarters, procured him help in stowing his gear, shook his hand to welcome him aboard, and ordered him to report to the commandant of the Station, Machine Colonel Mohammed Zafar.

Gann's assignment was to investigate rumors of strange

anti-Plan activities on the Polaris Station. Gann was a soldier of the Plan, and he could hardly conceive of anything anti-Plan that was not at the same time corrupt, slovenly, evil, and wrong. He had come to the station expecting to find it rundown and rusty, manned by surly malcontents.

Yet the discipline was good. The men were on their toes. On the way through the plastic passages of the wheel, stepping high in the light gravity of the station's spin, he saw that the metalwork was bright. Confusing, thought Gann, mildly perplexed; but he knew his duty and he knew how to do it.

He knocked on the door of the commandant's office and was ordered inside. He came to full attention and a brisk salute.

"Technicadet Gann reporting as ordered, sir!"

The Machine Colonel returned his salute methodically. Here, too, Gann was faintly surprised, though he allowed none of the surprise to show through his military bearing and engaging grin. Machine Colonel Zafar was a short brown man in meticulously pressed dress whites, who looked as solid and enduring as the Plan itself. "Welcome aboard, cadet," he said. "Give me your orders, please."

"Yes, sir!" Gann's orders were also a lie. They showed him to be a relief laser operator fresh out from Earth. They did not mention his true rank, or his intensive training on Pluto. The commandant read them carefully, then nodded.

"Cadet Gann," he said in his soft, precise voice, "we are glad to have you on Polaris Station. As you know, this station is a major unit in the Spacewall. Our primary job is to detect and intercept any unauthorized traffic between the Plan of Man and the areas beyond Pluto— the wastes that are called the Reefs of Space. Our secondary job is to monitor as much activity in the Reefs as possible. Our radar, laser, and optical systems are the heart of our mission—and so, Cadet Gann, what you do is the most important part of our work here. Don't fail us."

"Sir," said Boysie Gann earnestly, "I won't fail you! I serve the Plan of Man without question or pause!" And he saluted and left.

But before he left he dropped his orders and retrieved them, with a flashing grin of apology to the colonel.

He left with his shoulders high. For in the instant when he was bent out of the commandant's sight, picking up his papers, he had planted a listening bug under the projecting rim of Machine Colonel Zafar's desk.

Within an hour of Gann's arrival on Polaris Station he was fitted with an iron collar.

He had expected it. In so sensitive an installation as the station, every man wore one of the Machine's collars, so that at any instant, wherever he might be, any one of them could be destroyed. There was no other way. A space man gone amok—a traitor loose in the fuel stores —a drunken armorer at the studs of the station's mighty missiles—any individual could do so much harm that it was necessary to have instant control over every man aboard.

Still, it was an uncomfortable feeling. Gann touched the collar lightly, and for once the smile was gone from his cheerful face. It was disturbing to know that some-one somewhere—the distant Machine on Earth, or one of its satellites nearby, a security officer on Pluto, or the commandant here on the station—could at the surge of a radar pulse detonate the decapitation charge.

His bunkmate was a tall, lean Nigerian, Technicadet M'Buna. Lounging in the security office waiting for Gann, M'Buna saw his involuntary gesture and laughed. As he held the door and they started off to their duty post M'Buna said, "Makes you nervous, eh? Don't worry. If it goes off, you'll never know it!"

Gann grinned. He liked M'Buna, had at first encounter already realized that here was an intelligent, patient friend. Yet he said at once, "Nobody likes a collar. And—" he acted a pause, glancing around—"I hear there are people somewhere who do something about it. Out on the Reefs. Men who know how to get the collars off . . ."

M'Buna said uncomfortably, "I wouldn't know anything about that. Here's our station."

Gann nodded and let it pass. But he had not failed to notice that M'Buna had overlooked one essential act. What Gann said hinted at treason to the Plan. M'Buna's duty was clear: he should have called Gann on it and established exactly what was meant by the hint. . . . And then reported Gann at once.

Huge as an ocean liner, flimsy as a dragon kite, Polaris Station was a big plastic wheel. Its spin was just fast enough to keep the crew's soup in the plate and the plate on the table. The hub was stationary, with the radar-laser search dome on the north face, the entry locks on the other.

The station had been set up first, more than a quarter century before, as a base for exploring the Reef cluster immediately to the galactic north of the sun. The snowball that had supplied reaction mass for the old nuclear rockets was still in detector range, swinging a hundred miles from the station in their coupled orbits. Now there was no need for reaction mass, but the snow-asteroid still had its uses. It served as a cosmic garbage dump, the unreclaimed wastes and offal of the station hauled out there after every watch and left on its surface so that free-orbiting particles of trash would not return false signals to the search instruments back at the station.

Within forty-eight hours of reporting aboard the station, Machine Major Boysie Gann had bugged the offices of the commandant, the executive officer, the quartermaster, and the intelligence chief. Each tiny instrument was broadcasting a sealed-wave pickup of every word that was uttered in those sacrosanct chambers. Gann himself spot-monitored the transmissions when time allowed. The rest of the time the great records machine on Pluto received the signals, taped them, and transmitted them to Earth and the buried citadel of the Planning Machine itself.

But all his bugs produced nothing.

Gann's orders had been less than explicit: *Seek out and identify enemies of the Plan.* Beyond that there had been only rumors. A vast smuggling enterprise, shipping valuable strategic materials from the inner Plan Worlds to the Reefs. A strange new cult that threatened to unite the Reefs against the inner planets. A leader preaching a hegira, a security leak . . . But which of these was true, if any, Gann had not been told. It was not security doctrine to tell agents precisely what they should be looking for, on the grounds that their time was most productively employed when they could develop and follow up on many of their own leads.

Yet here there were no leads at all.

No real leads, at least. A few unguarded remarks at mess. Some slipshod accounting of spare parts for the laser banks. These were anti-Plan irregularities, to be sure, and men had gone to the Body Bank for far less. Men would go to the Body Bank for them now, from Polaris Station, for Gann had promptly filed the names and data. But he was certain that what he should be looking for was something bigger and worse than an occasional disgruntled or sloppy officer.

Within one week Gann had proved to his own satisfaction that if there was any major anti-Plan activity going on, it was not on Polaris Station.

He had to look elsewhere.

But where else was there?

It wasn't until he had been there twice that he realized where the "elsewhere" had to be.

Like all the noncommissioned personnel, Gann took his share of KP, garbage detail, cleanup orderly, and so on. It was not usually a burdensome chore. The radar ovens and cybernated housekeepers did all the work; the only thing left for the men in charge was to make sure they were working properly. Even the short hop from station to the snowball for garbage disposal was a welcome break in the routine.

He shared his garbage tour with M'Buna, and they spent their time chatting desultorily at the controls of the "scow"—actually a reactionless space tractor—while the garbage pods steered, unloaded, and returned themselves. M'Buna had never referred to Gann's leading remark about collars. Nor had Gann ever been able to draw him into any unplanned talk; he had given up trying. They talked about home. They talked about promotion. And they talked about girls.

For Gann there was one girl, and her name was Julie Martinet. "No bigger than a minute, M'Buna," he said earnestly, "and with those beautiful dark eyes. She's waiting for me. When I come back—"

"Sure," said M'Buna. "Now, this girl I knew in Lagos—"

"You're talking about *a* girl," said Gann. "Julie is *the* girl. The only one who matters."

"How come you never get any mail from her?" asked M'Buna.

And Gann froze.

"She doesn't like to write letters," he said after a

moment, but inside he was cursing himself. So foolish a slip! There was a reason, and a perfectly good one, why he got no letters from Julie Martinet. They were piling up for him on Pluto; he was sure of that; but they could not be forwarded here. There was too much risk of someone reading one, and learning from some chance comment that Gann was not the simple laser tech he appeared.

As soon as he could, Gann changed the subject. "Say," he said, "what's that on the scope?" It was a tiny blip, settling down feather-light toward the surface of the snowball protoplanet. A clutter of trash, of course. Nothing more. It was by no means unusual for some part of the garbage cargo to rebound from the tenuous clutch of the snowball's gravity and wheel around in space for minutes or hours before finally settling into place.

But M'Buna glanced at the radar display and said casually, "The commandant, I suppose. He comes out here every once in a while to check things over."

Carefully, trying to hide his excitement, Gann said, "Wonder what he does there." M'Buna shrugged, reached forward, and turned a switch. The pod had emptied itself and returned to the ship. "Tell you what," Gann went on. "Let's look."

He didn't wait for an answer. The pod back, the scow ready, there was nothing to stop him. He fed the ion stream to the reactionless drive and cut in the course-correcting side rockets. The scow began to move.

M'Buna said tautly, "No! Cut it out, Gann. The Old Man isn't going to want us skylarking around without permission."

But Gann wasn't listening. He was watching the screens intently.

If Machine Colonel Zafar was paying surreptitious visits to the ice-planetoid, there had to be a reason. He was going to find out what that reason was. He cut in maximum magnification on the screens, and the surface of the little protoplanet of frozen gases leaped up toward him.

The thing was eight or ten miles thick, shaped more like a broken cinder block than a sphere. It was unusually dense, as the distant, orbiting blobs of frozen methane and hydrogen went; if it ever drifted in near the sun, it would make a major comet. In the screen its greenish crust of solid gases looked like a blizzard in slow motion. Disturbed by the impact of the waste they had dumped, the whole snowball was quivering and shaking, its light gas-snow rising in sheets and falling again.

There was absolutely nothing to be seen . . .

But even a tiny planetoid has a great deal of surface, by human standards. Somewhere on that surface Colonel Zafar had gone in his flying suit. Gann reached again for the controls to circle around.

Some noise warned him.

He turned, and saw M'Buna leaning toward him, a strange expression of mingled pity and hate on his face; and in M'Buna's hand was a glittering metal pencil, pointed at him.

In that split second of time that was left to him Gann thought wildly: *If only I could get the report in, I've sure found something anti-Plan going on now* . . .

And that was the last thought he had for a long time. He heard a hiss and just had time to realize that the sting on his cheek was a nerve pellet fired from M'Buna's contraband gun. That was all. Blackness closed over him, and cold.

III

A nerve pellet is an instant anesthetic. It is also something more.

It does not wear off. Not ever. The victim of a nerve pellet does not recover consciousness until he is given an antidote.

When Gann woke up, he had no idea of how long he had been under the influence of the nerve pellet. But what he knew for sure was that he was no longer in the control room of the garbage scow.

Nor was he anywhere else in the universe where he had ever been before.

He lay on an uneven, rocky ledge. Under him was a soft, moist—and warm—blanket of something that seemed to be a lichen, a kind of clinging moss that grew in thick, flaky scales. It was glowing with a soft steady light. On the rocks around him the light was greenish in hue. Farther away, on higher ridges, it shone purple and red.

And above the rocks the sky was velvet black, with a single dazzling star blazing down on him.

Boysie Gann struggled to his feet—and soared into the air.

As he came down he stared about him. When he looked away from the rocks and that bright star his eyes adjusted and he could see other stars. All the familiar constellations . . . And then it hit him.

That bright star was the sun.

He was on one of the Reefs of Space.

Gann never knew how he came there. The man who would surely know was M'Buna, and Gann never saw M'Buna again. But it was clear that while under the influence of the nerve pellet he had been transported and marooned. Alone, without a radio, without instruments, without a ship or spacesuit, he might live out his life on that Reef—but he would die there in the end. For he could never leave.

It was surely a good way to dispose of an unwanted man—simpler even than murder, since there was no body to get rid of.

He was stiff and cold. His wrists were swollen and his ankles numb. Evidently his captors had not trusted to the nerve pellet to keep him quiet, but had shackled him as well. But the shackles were gone now, with every other evidence of who it was who had brought him here. His head hurt. He was parched and hungry.

He began to look around him more methodically.

His first needs were food and water; but he could not resist a look around at the wonder of the place. Bright metallic fern fronds tinkled like wind gongs from an overgrown vale to one side. A distant whirring sounded like a flock of grouse. Impossible that there should be grouse here, Gann knew; yet there might be some sort of life. The Reefs of Space were created by life, like the coral atolls on Earth's warm seas. Life inhabited them all . . .

But it was not always—not even often!—life of a sort compatible with humankind. For the Reefs were formed from clusters of fusorians, feasting on the hydrogen formed between the stars according to the laws of the Neo-Hoyle Hypothesis, converting it into heavier atoms, then into atoms heavier still. The life in the Reefs was sometimes warm-blooded, carbon-based, oxygen-breathing animal. But more often it was metal or crystal—at best, worthless for food; at worst, a deadly danger.

The bright star Sol was near the south celestial pole, Gann discovered. That put him more or less galactic north of the sun—and, therefore, almost straight out from Polaris Station. How far out? He had no way of knowing, except that the major Reef clusters were thought to be some two hundred astronomical units from Sol. At a guess, twenty billion miles.

Gann turned his eyes from the stars and looked about him. He had a world to explore. It might be less than a hundred yards in its longest axis, but it was all he had.

He rubbed his aching wrists and ankles and began to explore. He climbed carefully out of that small, glowing green dell—carefully, because he knew the danger of a reeflet. The fusorian symbiotes held an atmosphere, somehow; but it was like a soap bubble, and if Gann was so incautious as to step too high and soar through it, he would find himself in the hard vacuum of the space between the stars, and death would come in a horrible explosive burst as his blood boiled off and his cells ruptured.

He climbed toward the ridge, paused, and looked around.

Ahead of him was another dell, this one bearing some sort of glittering bush. The plants were shoulder-high, with plumes of narrow gloss, sprinkled with what seemed to be individual fusorian cells that glowed with their own light. Each leaf darkened from green at the base to black at the tip, and each ended in a bright red berry.

Queerly, they grew in rows.

They looked, in fact, like a truck farm in Earth's populous market valleys, and at once Gann's hunger surged forth. They looked like food! He started toward them at a shambling run . . .

And from behind him a voice spoke. "Well, good for you. See you woke up finally. Headed right for the feed-bag too, eh?"

Machine Major Boysie Gann's training had prepared him for any shock. It was trained reflex that stopped him in midflight, turned him, brought him back down to the glowing mossy surface of the reeflet in a half crouch, ready to do battle.

But there was nothing warlike in the figure that was coming toward him. He was a stubby little man with a big belly and a dirty yellow beard. His clothing was woven out of some kind of rough fiber. It was ragged and filthy and half unbuttoned.

And clinging to his bald brown head was a black-fanged, green-scaled, red-eyed creature the size of a capuchin monkey. It looked like a toy dragon. And from under the knife-sharp edges of its scales seeped little wisps of smoke.

Boysie Gann said warily, "Hello."

"Why, hello," the man said in a mild voice. "You was sleeping. Figured I'd best leave you to sleep it off. Nice to have you here. I wasn't expecting company."

"I wasn't exactly expecting to be here."

The man nodded and thrust out a dirty, gnarled hand. "Figured that. Couple fellows dropped you five, six hours ago. Looks like they gave you a rough enough time, so I let you be."

The creature on its head wheeled to face Gann as its owner moved, glaring at him with hot red eyes. Gann shook the man's hand and said, "I need some water. And food."

"Why, sure. Come along then." He nodded, the creature scrambling back and forth, and turned to lead the way across the cultivated field toward what seemed to be a tiny black lake. "Omer don't like strangers," he called over his shoulder, "but he won't bother you none. Just don't make any sudden moves is all. Omer's a pyropod —just a baby, of course, but they can be mean."

Silently Gann agreed. The little creature looked mean enough, with its oozing plumes of smoke and fiery eyes. They loped across the glowing rows of the man's little farm and reached the shore of the lake—no more than a pond, really, fifty feet across, its surface disturbed with the slow, tall waves of low-gravity fluids. On its far bank a sharp cliff rose in a glitter of metallic outcroppings, softened by glowing plants and mosses, and in the base of the cliff was a metal lean-to that hid the mouth of the cave.

"That's home," said the man cheerfully. "Welcome to it, such as 'tis. Come in and rest yourself."

"Thanks," said Gann. "By the way, we didn't really introduce ourselves."

"Oh? Guess you're right," said the man. "I'm Harry Hickson. And you"—Gann started to speak, but Hickson didn't pause—"you're what you call it—Machine Major Boysie Gann, out of the spy school on Pluto."

For twenty-four hours, Gann rested in the cave of the hermit Harry Hickson, and his thoughts were dark. How had Hickson known his name? Even more, how had he known that he was not a shanghaied radar-laser tech, but a graduate of the spy school?

There was no answer in Gann's brain, so he shut off his mind to conjectures and applied it to restoring his physical condition and reconnoitering his surroundings.

Evidently he had been unconscious for longer than he had thought on the ship that had dumped him on this reeflet, for he had lost weight and strength and there was a straggly stubble of beard on his chin. But Hickson fed him and cared for him. He gave Gann a bed of sorts to sleep on—only a stack of reeking blankets, but as good as the one he slept on himself—and fed him from the same pot of greasy stew as himself. The diet was crude but filling, supplemented with fruits and roots and shoots of the plants he grew on the rock. The reddish berries, which tasted like a sort of acid citrus fruit, were a good source of all necessary vitamins, Harry told him earnestly, and one of the lichens was a source of protein.

Gann did not question the food. Clearly it had kept Harry Hickson alive for a long time—the cave showed that it had been his home for months or even years— and it would keep Gann alive for at least as long as he intended to stay on the reeflet.

And that would not be long. For he had learned from Hickson that there was a way of communicating that would bring help if he needed it. "Never needed it, o' course," he said, fishing a long string of a rhubarb-like vegetable out of his bowl of stew and licking his fingers. "But it's comforting to know it's there . . . Say, you worried about that collar, Boysie?"

Gann stopped in mid-gesture, suddenly aware that he had been tugging at it. "Not exactly," he said quietly.

"Get it off of you, if you like," Hickson offered mildly. "No trouble. Done it lots o' times."

Gann stared. "What the Plan are you talking about?" he demanded. "Don't you know what this is? These things are built with automatic destruct circuits, as well as the remote triggering equipment. If anybody tries to take them off—" He touched both sides of the collar with fingertips and flipped them up and outward, pantomiming the explosion of a decapitation charge.

"Oh, sure, I know all about *that*," said Hickson. "Hold still. No, not you, Gann. *You,* Omer! Don't wiggle so. Makes me nervous."

He got up from his squatting position at the rude plank table where they ate and came around behind Gann.

"Just you sit there, Boysie," he said. "Can move if you want to—it don't matter—but don't look toward me . . . Omer, confound you! Get your claws outa my scalp! Raised him from an egg, that little devil, right here in my own smoke pot, but he gets jumpy when he knows I'm going to . . . Well, here we are."

And something moved around Gann's neck. He couldn't see what Hickson was doing, was sure that the tubby little hermit had not brought any tools or instruments. Yet there was a sudden constriction at his throat.

He heard the lock snap . . .

The collar fell off his neck and clattered to the floor of the cave. Gann leaped to his feet and spun, white-faced, to be ready for the explosion. But no explosion came.

"Now, rest easy, Boysie," complained the hermit. "You're spooking Omer here. That thing can't blow up any more." Casually he picked up the collar and lifted it to examine it in the light of a mass of luminous diamond that would have been worth millions on earth. "They make them real nice," he said admiringly. "Lot of detail in this thing. Too bad it can't be something more useful." And he tossed it to the rear of the cave. "Well," he said, "you about ready to move on now?"

Gann stood silent for a second, looking at him. "Move on where?" he asked.

"Oh, don't worry, Boysie. I know what you were thinking. Plain as day. You figure I ought to go back and get examined by the Planning Machine, 'cause you don't quite understand what I'm up to, but you think it's unplanned. Well, that's right. Unplanned is what I am. And I don't mind if you do what you're thinking, and take my laser-gun and call help so you can get out of here. But I'm not going with you, Boysie. Make up your mind to that."

"All right," said Gann, surrendering. But in his mind he was not surrendering at all.

Hickson had put it very mildly when he said that Gann wanted to take him back for study. Gann not only wanted to; he intended to. In fact, he had never intended anything as hard in his life—had never been so determined or insistent, not even about his career in the service of the Machine, not even in his great love for Julie Martinet.

This man Harry Hickson was an unplanned disaster in the making.

Whoever he was, however he did what he did, he was a terrible danger to the Plan of Man. Gann could almost hear the instructions of his briefing officer back on Pluto —if he had been able to report Hickson's existence to him, and if the briefing officer could issue an order: *Subject Hickson is a negative factor. His uncatalogued knowledge must be retrieved for the Plan. Then each organ of his unautomated body must be obliterated . . .*

But how to get him back into the jurisdiction of the Planning Machine?

There had to be a way. There would be a way. Machine Major Boysie Gann was sure of it. All it required was that he be patient—then, when his chance came, be ready.

Gann said, "If you mean it, then let's take your gun and signal right now. I'm ready to move on."

Harry Hickson led Gann to a point of red-scaled rock, puffing and wheezing. On his bald scalp the fledgling pyropod wheeled and slithered, keeping its bright red eyes on Boysie Gann.

"See up there?" called Hickson over his shoulder. "That star there next to Vega . . ."

Boysie Gann followed his pointing finger. "You mean Theta Lyrae?"

The hermit turned and looked at him, mildly surprised. "That's right, Boysie. You fellows learn a lot in that spy school. Too bad you don't . . . Well, never mind that.

One I mean, it's just below Theta Lyrae. The faint red one. Forget the name, but that one right there. That way's Freehaven."

Gann felt his blood pound. "Freehaven? I've heard of it. A colony of reef rats."

"Aw, Boysie, don't say it like that. They're free men —that's all. That's the biggest place in the Reefs, Freehaven is. Like a . . . well, what would you call it? A kind of a town only it's one whole cluster of Reefs, maybe a hundred thousand miles across. And maybe half a billion miles from here."

"I see," said Gann, thinking with exultation and pride, *What a prize to bring back to Pluto! A whole city to be planned and returned to the brotherhood of the Machine!* He could almost see the glowing jet trails of the Plan cruisers vectoring in on the cluster . . .

"Don't get your hopes up," Hickson said dryly. "You ain't there yet, Boysie, and maybe even when you get there you won't find it too easy to pick up a phone and call the Machine. Now hush a minute while I send for your ride out there."

He picked up the clumsy old laser gun he had taken out of its greasy rag wrappings back in the cave, checked its power settings, raised it, and aimed carefully at the distant red spark that was the line-of-sight to Freehaven. Three times he snapped the trigger, then lowered the gun and turned to Gann.

"That's all there is to it. Take 'em a while to get here. Might as well go back to the cave."

But he paused, glancing at Boysie Gann as if he was mildly embarrassed about something. Then he seemed to come to a decision.

He turned back to the stars, set down the laser pistol, and stretched out his arms. His lips moved, but Gann could hear no sound. On his bald pate the pyropod hissed and slithered. The hermit's whole body seemed stretched, yearning, toward—toward what?

Gann could not tell. Toward Freehaven, perhaps. Toward the faint red star that marked its position—or toward Theta Lyrae nearby—or toward the great bright giants of the Summer Triangle that marked that part of the sky, Vega, Altair, and Deneb . . .

Then Harry Hickson relaxed and the pyropod scuttled down from his scalp onto his shoulder as the hermit raised one arm and made a sinuous, undulating motion. Like the wriggle of a snake, Gann thought. Or the looping movement of a swan's neck.

Swan? Some faint old memory stirred in Boysie Gann's mind. Something about a swan—and a star . . .

But it would not come clear, and he followed Harry Hickson back to the cave.

Harry Hickson's little reeflet was one drifting island in an expanding infinity of matter and space. The doctrine of the Neo-Hoyle Hypothesis was clear: The universe was limitless, in space, in time—and in matter. New mass was forming everywhere in the form of newly created hydrogen atoms as the old complexes of matter—the stars and the planets, the dust clouds and the galaxies—were spinning slowly apart.

Hickson's reeflet was an infant among bodies of organized matter, probably only a few millions of years in age, in size no more than a dust mote. Yet it was like most of the universe in that; for most matter is young. The spiraling growth in rate of creation of new matter makes that sure. Some galaxies, and even some of the reefs between them, are old beyond computation and imagination, because the steady-state universe has neither beginning nor end. And life is the oldest phenomenon of all. Older than the oldest stars—but yet young, though those scattered and forgotten stars are black and dead.

Life in space has lived—literally—forever.

Every possible biology has been evolved, through every conceivable evolutionary test.

Watching Harry Hickson play with his pet pyropod, Boysie Gann reflected that the strangest life form he knew was man. For here was the pudgy, balding hermit—unplanned and deviant, a deadly danger by every standard of the Planning Machine—solemnly attempting to teach his pyropod to fly.

He lifted the little horror off his head and set it carefully on a high ledge, then retreated. Spitting and hissing, its red eyes glittering, its scales seeping the smoke of its internal jet fires, it wailed in a thin, raucous screech for him to come back. Then, despairing, it launched itself out into the air, missed Hickson by yards and crashed into the rock wall at the far side of the cave, where it remained, writhing and hissing, until Hickson took pity on it and picked it up. "It's a wonder it doesn't dash its brains out," muttered Gann the fifth time the little beast crashed into the rock.

"Oh, I guess so," Hickson agreed mildly. "Don't suppose it has any, really, though. A pretty clumsy kind of beast it is—right, Omer?" And he patted the little monster with the appearance of real affection for a moment, then sighed and set it down. He carefully inverted a crate and set it down over the pyropod, then put a mass of silvery fusorian coral upon the crate.

The pyropod squalled and hissed, but Hickson ignored it. "Hoped I could teach it to fly before I go," he said regretfully, "but I guess I won't make it. Boysie, your transportation ought to be here in an hour. Care to see what the pilot's gonna look like?" He thumbed an old-fashioned two-dimensional color print out of a button-down pocket in his ragged coat and handed it to Gann. It was a pretty, quite young girl, one hand resting on the head of a seal-like creature, before a background of a glowing purple and silver Reef. "Name's Quarla," said the old man affectionately. "Quarla Snow. Daughter of an old friend of mine. He treated me, couple years ago. Doctor, he is, and a good one. Don't know much about what ails me, though . . ."

The hermit seemed to realize he was rambling and caught himself up short. "Guess that's all," he said, smiling with a touch of embarrassment. "Swan bless you, Boysie. Give Quarla my love." And in a moment, before Gann could realize what he was about to do, the old man had turned, pushed aside the metal door that overhung the entrance to the cave, and stepped out.

Gann shook his head, half in rueful amusement, half in surprise. "Hey!" he called. "Hickson! Where are you going? Wait for me!" And he hurried to the door of the cave and out onto the sward the old hermit had so carefully cropped.

The man was not there.

His footprints were there, still visible in the faint bruises on the lichenous surface of the earth.

But Harry Hickson was gone.

Gann ranged the surface of the entire reef in the next few hours, shouting and searching. But there was no answer to his call, no sight of Hickson anywhere.

The man had simply vanished.

IV

In the cave Machine Major Gann found the old man's laser gun—an ancient Technicorps model that must have been smuggled into space before the Spacewall was set up. It gave him a small feeling of confidence to carry it, though there was no visible enemy to shoot it at.

He needed that confidence.

No man can be alone. Each man has his place in the Plan of Man under the benevolent guidance of the Planning Machine. Each man serves the Plan, so that the Plan may serve all men . . .

That was doctrine, and Boysie Gann found himself foolishly repeating it as he clambered up the red-scaled rock to the point from which Hickson had signaled to Freehaven. It did not help very much.

No man can be alone . . . but Boysie Gann felt very much alone indeed, on that tiny floating islet of reef, under the blazing stare of a billion stars.

There was no reason for him to be on this point of rock, rather than anywhere else on the surface of the reeflet. He had no reason to believe his rescuer would come to look for him there. Had no reason to be sure there would be a rescuer at all, in fact, for what the half-demented hermit, Harry Hickson, had said could not be accepted as reliable . . .

Yet he stayed there, waiting, for hours. He leaned

against a cairn of rock and scanned the skies. Only the distant, unfriendly stars returned his look. He sat, leaning against the rock, and drowsed. No sound or motion disturbed him. Then . . .

There was a faint blur of greenish mist in the low black sky, moving at the threshold of vision.

Gann sprang to his feet, eyes peering into the immense emptiness above him. The greenish blur was so faint that he could not be sure it was real. Yet . . . surely there was something there and, following it, a cluster of even fainter reddish sparks.

Gann raised the laser, checked the settings to make sure he was not firing a blast of destruction into the sky, and thumbed the trigger thrice, as he had seen Hickson do, pointing it toward the greenish blur.

A moment . . . then the green glow veered toward him.

It was his rescuer—he was sure of it. But what were the red sparks? Even as he watched, the tiny, distant coals veered too, following the greenish glow. Rapidly they grew nearer . . .

Then one of the red sparks dashed ahead of the rest, with a long blue trail of incandescence faintly visible behind it. It was like an ominous comet as it dived through the greenish cloud.

Noise smote Gann's ears abruptly: a sudden roaring, like the jet of an old-time rocket.

The things had come at last into the shallow atmosphere of his reeflet. He heard the shriek of their motion through the air—and something else.

Something was screaming.

The red spark thundered overhead, out of the green cloud, toward Gann like some deadly ancient missile homing in on a radar trace—then at the last moment rose up a dozen yards above his head, and as it passed he caught a sudden glimpse of nightmare.

Metal scales like broken mirrors. Enormous talons,

dripping something that glowed and was golden, something that splattered to the ground near Gann like a soft, fitful rain. The red spark divided into two red, monstrous, blinking eyes, mirror-rimmed, in a head like a maniac dragon's. And the roaring blue flame was the tail of the thing.

"Pyropod!" breathed Boysie Gann aloud, transfixed.

He had never seen an adult before—had heard of them only as distant rumors, like the sort of ghost stories unplanned parents used to tell their children. The baby pyropod that had been Harry Hickson's pet had not prepared him for the huge, menacing reality that shrieked through the air above him now. He stood, stunned.

A pyropod is a living rocket, flame-footed and deadly. Their chemistry is not that of Earthly air-breathers; their primeval genesis came from the same noncarbon evolutionary strain that shaped the fusorians. On their plasma jets, nuclear in temperature, fired by fusorian symbiotes, they can outrun a Plan cruiser and outfight any Terrestrial beast in search of prey. And to the pyropods, anything that moves is prey. Their jets take enormous quantities of reaction mass. Their appetites are insatiable. Scavengers of space, they will attack anything.

Fortunately for the continuation of life on the inner planets and the Reefs of Space, atmosphere is a slow poison to the pyropods and gravity damages their reflexes. They are beasts of the interstellar void, ship-sized monstrosities at their hugest, big as cave bears even when barely mature. Standing in shock, watching the great beast, Boysie Gann stared at the red eyes pulsing in their telescopic mirrors, wheel and flash back toward him, imagined the black talons ripping metal or rock like bread . . .

And realized, almost too late, that he was the target of those monstrous talons now.

Instinctively he raised the laser gun and fired.

The charge was minimal, only the message setting; yet

the great pyropod felt it, screamed, and soared away. Gann hurled himself to the shelter of the rock cairn, staring about. The torn green cloud of luminosity was dissolving in the night sky above him. Streamers of mist scattered and faded. And where the cloud had been, Gann could see what had brought it.

A spaceling. One of the warm-blooded, seal-like creatures that roam the space between the stars, natural prey to the pyropods, friend to man. It had brought the cloud —for it was the spaceling's ability to hold atmosphere about it, in a Ryeland-effect field, that permitted them, as oxygen-breathers, to live in space at all.

The spaceling had been grievously wounded. Even from so far away, Gann could see the hideous slash that ripped along the whole length of its sleek, golden body as it came tumbling down. Something was clinging to its fur —a rider? Gann could not be sure; but what he was certain of was that the end for both the spaceling and its burden was very near.

The pyropod that had attacked him had wheeled again and was diving on the wounded seal-like beast. A louder howling drowned out the spaceling's scream as the pyropod came out of the dark over a purple-scaled ridge, red eyes pulsing and dripping talons reaching again.

Gann reacted without thought. He twisted the crystal of that old laser to maximal intensity, steadied the tube on the rocks of the cairn, and fired into those dreadful flashing eyes. They exploded.

The pyropod bellowed in agony. Its eyes were gone —eyes or eyelike structures; actually, Gann knew, they were more like laser search gear. But whatever they were, they were gone now, burst like the shattered hull of a subtrain when the field of its tunnel fails and the fluid rock crushes it. The pyropod drove blindly up and away, squalling until its sound was cut off like the dropping of a curtain.

It had passed beyond the atmosphere into space. Blind and wounded, it would not, Gann thought, be back. And a blessing that was, since an orange light was blinking on the laser gun, warning him that the fuel cell was fully exhausted.

He knew there were other pyropods still out there, somewhere beyond the veil of air. He could see their faint red sparks circling, and the blue trails of their fiery exhausts. They veered all at once, and drove in toward the retreating comet tail of the pyropod he had wounded. There was a puff of incandescent vapor . . .

Dimly Gann realized that its mates had destroyed the wounded one, torn it open and were now wheeling and diving, fighting for their shares of the kill. But he had no time for them. The spaceling had tumbled to earth halfway across the little reeflet, and Gann stumbled and leaped across the red-scaled rocks to find it.

It was lying at the edge of Harry Hickson's little plantation, spurting glowing yellow blood across the green moss. Beside it was its rider, bent over the terrible wound, trying with both hands to stanch the flow of blood.

The rider was a girl. Hickson had been right. It was the girl in the photograph he had displayed.

The spaceling moaned and shuddered as Gann drew near, its voice a faint, inarticulate sob. The girl was sobbing too.

"Can I help?" said Boysie Gann.

The girl, Quarla Snow, turned quickly, startled. She stared at Gann as if he were himself a pyropod, or some more fearsome monster from legend. There was fright in her eyes—and yet, queerly, thought Gann, almost relief as well, as if she had expected something even worse. It was the expression of a man who finds himself confronted by a wolf, when he expects a tiger.

"Who are you?" she demanded. Her voice was low and controlled. She was tall and strong, but very young.

"Boysie Gann," he said. "And you're Quarla Snow. Harry Hickson told me you'd be here."

Her hand flew to her mouth. Her eyes widened in fear. For a moment she seemed about to run; then she shook her head in a pathetic gesture and turned back to the spaceling.

Its golden blood had ceased to flow, its body to move. The sounds it had uttered were still.

"Sultana's dead," the girl said softly, as if to herself.

"I'm sorry," Boysie Gann said inadequately. He glanced aloft—the pyropods were out of sight entirely now—then back to her. Quarla Snow's face was lightly tanned, almost to match her honey-colored hair. She was nearly the color of her spaceling. Her white coveralls were splashed with that golden ichor, her hands dripping with it. Yet she was beautiful.

For a moment a buried emotion trembled inside Boysie Gann, a memory of Julie Martinet and the taste of the fresh salt surf on her mouth when he kissed her on the beach of the little Mexican resort, Playa Blanca, long ages ago when they had said good-by. This girl did not in the least resemble Julie Martinet. She was blond where Julie had hair like night; she was tall, and Julie tiny. Her face was broad, friendly, and even in her sorrow and fear it showed contentment and joy in life, while Julie Martinet was a girl of sad pleasures and half-expressed sorrows. Yet there was something in both of them that stirred him.

He said hastily, "Those things may be back. We'd better do something about it."

The girl's tears were drying on her cheeks and her expression had become more calm. She looked down at the dead gun in Gann's hands and half smiled. "Not with that, Boysie Gann. It's empty."

"I know. We'd better get back to Hickson's cave. He may have left other charges."

"Left them? But I thought you said he was here!" The shadow fell over her face again, her eyes bright and fearful.

"He was, yes. But he's gone. Disappeared. I don't know where."

The girl nodded absently, as if she were too dazed to take in what he had said. She dropped to her knees beside the dead spaceling and stroked its golden head. "Poor Sultana. I'll never forgive myself. When I got your signal I . . . well, I was frightened. I didn't know what to do. Dad was gone on an emergency call. He'd taken our ship, and . . . I decided to ride Sultana out here by myself."

Her mouth set white for a moment. "I didn't really think of any danger. There aren't many pyropods in these clusters any more—been hunted out years ago, though they keep straying back. But I'd outrun them on Sultana often enough before. I didn't think about the fact that she's . . . that she was . . . getting old."

She stood up and touched Gann lightly on the arm, a gesture of reassurance. "But you're not to worry. We aren't marooned here; Dad will come for us in the ship as soon as he gets home. I left a message."

Gann nodded. "So he'll wait a while," he said, comprehendingly, "and then, if you haven't returned in—what? a day or so? Then he'll come looking for you."

But Quarla Snow shook her golden head, her expression unreadable. "No. He won't wait. Not even a second. I said in my note that Harry Hickson's old distress signal had come. He'll be here as fast as his ship can bring him, to see who sent Harry's signal."

Gann stared. "Harry did. Harry Hickson. I told you!"

"I know you told me," the girl said, her voice calm but with an undercurrent of wonder and of fear. "But you see, it couldn't have been Harry. I—no, wait. I'll show you."

And she turned and led him away from the cultivated little field, back up to the red-scaled crest of rock, where he had rested his laser gun on the cairn of rocks to fire at the pyropod. "See?" she said, touching the cairn.

He bent closer to look, and there on the lowermost rock, on one half-smoothed face of a boulder, was a faint scratching of carved letters, whittled out a line at a time with a laser gun, almost invisible unless you knew just where to look:

Harry Hickson
Died of a fusorian infection
Deneb light his way

"You see?" said the girl. "Harry could not have sent the message. He died here three years ago."

V

All this was months before the Writ of Liberation. On Earth the old Planner sat in silent, joyous communion with the Planning Machine. In solarian space the great Plan cruisers arrowed from satellite to planet, from asteroid to distant Spacewall post, carrying the weapons and the orders of the Machine to all the far-flung territories of the Plan of Man. On the island of Cuba, in the Body Bank, a Nigerian ex-Technicorps man, broken for inefficiency, gave up the last of his vital organs to serve some more worthy servant of the Plan, and died. (His name had once been M'Buna. He had been captured and court-martialed for desertion.) A girl named Julie Martinet, in a dormitory hall far below the surface of the Peruvian Andes, sat with stylus in hand deciding on which letter to write—one to the man she loved "but had not heard from"; the other an application for special duty in the service of the Machine.

And out on the Reefs, in the sprawling hundred-orbed community called Freehaven, Machine Major Boysie Gann began to understand that his greatest opportunity for service—and his greatest hope of reward!—had been handed to him on a silver platter.

For he was at large in Freehaven, the very heart of the Reefs of Space. And he knew, or thought he knew, a way to get back to the worlds of the Plan.

True, there were some puzzling problems. Some of them, indeed, were almost frightening.

What could Quarla Snow hope to gain by pretending that Harry Hickson was dead? What did she think Gann had seen on the little reeflet? A ghost? It was no ghost that had fed him, healed him, taken the collar from around his neck.

And it was no coincidence, he was coming to believe, that had brought him to Hickson's world in the first place.

There was no proof, of course. But he was sure that M'Buna, perhaps Colonel Zafar as well, was in some way related to Hickson and the treasonable activities that were going on all around him in this unplanned, decadent, dangerous world of the Reefs. He had heard hints. An unguarded word, a look, a remark that was halted before it began. Nothing tangible, but enough to make him sure that there were links between the Reefs and the Plan worlds—links that extended even into the Technicorps, even into the vital defenses of the Spacewall itself.

If he could get back— No! he thought. *When* he got back, with the proof of this spreading rot, with the names of the conspirators and the evidence that would send them to the Body Bank, then no reward in the Machine's power would be too great to give to Machine Major Boysie Gann. And Julie Martinet would be waiting. . . .

Meanwhile there was a lot of work to do.

Gann dared not make notes or attempt to secure tapes or photographs; but he missed no opportunity to scout and examine every part of this queer community of Freehaven. Even the name was strange and somehow disconcerting. Freehaven.

As if "freedom" were important!

Yet Boysie Gann could not help but notice that strangely the decadent, unruly mobs that dwelt in Freehaven seemed somehow sturdier, somehow happier, in some way more alert and even more prosperous than the billions who lived under the all-powerful and protective embrace of the Plan of Man. . . .

It was confusing.

But his duty was clear. Gann set himself to learn all there was to know.

Freehaven consisted of a couple of thousand people, scattered over a hundred fusorian-grown rocks and a hundred thousand miles of space. Many of the rocks had been terraformed, Gann learned, with the lichenous air plant he had first seen on Harry Hickson's little reef. The rest of them were airless, but all of them supplied useful metals and minerals to the bustling economy of Freehaven.

Gann was not sure just what he had expected—tattooed savages, perhaps, dancing to a wild tomtom—but he had surely not been prepared for this modern, busy community. There were farms and herds—of spacelings and even, in one case, a stock farm with sixty head of what seemed to be Guernsey cattle, stolen somehow from the Plan of Man and transported in some improbable manner out to this hydrogen-based worldlet twenty billion miles from the sun. On one airless reef that was mostly pure fusorian iron was a steel mill—one of the small nuclear-powered units developed by Technicorps engineers for use on the asteroids, to save the high cost of lifting terrain steel into space. Gann marveled at it all. He admitted it to Quarla Snow and her father, with whom he was staying as guest—or prisoner, he was never sure which—at a meal when he was served as fine a steak as he had ever tasted, with wines that bore the bouquet of French vineyards.

Dr. Snow boomed, "It isn't only the food that is good here, young man. It is life! It has a flavor here that the Plan worlds will never taste."

Boysie Gann said engagingly, "You may be right. I . . . well, you have to excuse me. You see, I've never known anything but the Plan."

Quarla's father nodded briskly. "Of course. None of us had, before we made our way out here. None but Quarla, at any rate, and a few others like her who were born here. They've lived in freedom all their lives."

Gann said, with just the right inflexion of doubt, "But I don't understand. I mean, how does it work? Who tells you what you're to do?"

"No one, boy! That's the whole point of freedom! We came here because we didn't want to live under the collar of the Machine. We work together, and as you see we work well. Prosperity and happiness! That's what we've built out of nothingness, just as the fusorians build our worlds for us out of thin gas and energy. Why, when Harry Hickson and I came here—" He broke off and tugged at his chin, frowning at Boysie Gann.

"Yes?" said Gann. "You and Hickson . . ."

"It was different then," said Dr. Snow shortly. "Boy, do you still want us to believe that story of yours about Hickson? A man I helped to bury myself, right under the rocks of his home?"

Gann said carefully, knowing that he was on dangerous ground, "Well, sir, of course I don't know anything about Hickson. But what I told you was true. The man who summoned Quarla said he was Harry Hickson, and I had absolutely no reason at all to doubt him at the time."

Snow nodded somberly and said no more; but Gann noticed that he no longer seemed to enjoy his meal.

Gann put the matter from his mind. He was thinking of something bigger. He was thinking of the gratitude of the Machine when he returned, riding one of Quarla Snow's spacelings—as she was even now teaching him to do—bringing word of the community of Freehaven and its precious crop of several thousand splendid candidates for tissue salvage at the Body Bank!

He rose and strolled outside with Quarla. Harry Hickson's pet pyropod, which Quarla had insisted on rescuing from the cave when her father arrived to take them off the reeflet, hissed and slithered around the area outside the door where its staked chain permitted it to move.

He took her hand and held it, as they looked over the green ramble of glowing vines toward the distant beacon that was the central urban area of Freehaven. "You promised to let me ride one of your spacelings," he said, squeezing her hand and grinning. "If I'm going to be a permanent inhabitant here, I'd better start learning my way around."

She looked at him thoughtfully, then smiled. Under her golden hair her eyes were an intense blue. "Why not?" she said. "But not out of the atmosphere, Boysie. Not at first."

"I thought the spacelings brought their air with them."

She nodded but said firmly, "Not out of the atmosphere. For one thing, there might be pyropods."

He scoffed, "So close to Freehaven? Nonsense, Quarla! What's the other thing?"

She hesitated. "Well," she began. She was saved the trouble of answering. A pale blue wash of energy brightened up the sky over their heads.

Both of them turned to look; a spacecraft was coming in for a landing, full jets blazing to slow its racing drive. Whoever it was who was piloting the craft, he was in a hurry. In a matter of seconds the ship was down on the lichenous lawn before Dr. Snow's clinic, its lock open, a man leaping out. He glanced toward Quarla and Boysie Gann, cried, "Emergency!" and turned to receive something that was being handed to him out the lock of the ship.

Quarla cried, "I'll get my father. Boysie, run and help

them!" Gann was already in motion, hurtling across the lichenous ground, though the two men in the rocket needed little help. What was coming through the lock of the ship was a man on a stretcher, wrapped in white sheets. In the light gravity of the Reef the two of them were perfectly adequate to handle it. Gann bore a hand anyway.

"Sick," panted one of the men. "Don't know who he is, but he collapsed in my spaceling corral. Thought it might be something dangerous—"

Gann nodded, helped lift the stretcher on which the sick man was thrashing and babbling . . .

And almost dropped it, light gravity or not.

He stood there, jaw hanging, eyes wide. Face streaming with perspiration, eyes vacant, head tossing from side to side in delirium, the face of the man on the stretcher was nevertheless very familiar to Boysie Gann. It was the face of Machine Colonel Mohammed Zafar.

If ever Boysie Gann had needed all the wits and wiles that had been drummed into him in the spy school on Pluto, now was the moment. "Dangerous," the reef rat who had brought Zafar had called him. He was more than dangerous; he spelled a strong probability of disaster for Boysie Gann. Zafar of all people would know him —and if, as Gann was morally certain, Zafar and M'Buna had been joined in some anti-Plan scheme on Polaris Station, Zafar would surely now know that Gann was no simple radar tech.

He dared not risk Zafar's recovering consciousness and identifying him. Yet his every loyalty to the Plan of Man demanded that he take every chance to learn more about Zafar from the colonel's disjointed ravings.

Dr. Snow made it easy for him, without knowing it. "You, boy!" he snapped. "Stay out of here. Quarla too!

May be contagious . . . But stay where I can find you if I need you," he added, bending over his patient.

The two of them stood at the door of the emergency room, Quarla's hand, forgotten, in Boysie Gann's. "He's bad, Boysie," she whispered. "Don't know what it is. I haven't seen anything like that since Harry—" Then she stopped, and went on, in a different tone, to the men who had brought him: "You'd better wait until my father's examined him. You might have been exposed."

In the emergency room Dr. Snow was lifting a bimetal thermometer out of Zafar's slack, mumbling mouth. Boysie Gann strained to hear what the man was saying, but all he could catch were words like ". . . trap for minds . . ." ". . . living dust and lying dreams . . ."

Dr. Snow's expression was serious. "High," he muttered, then glanced toward the group at the door. "Quarla!" he called. "You'll have to compound an injection for me. Standard broad-spectrum antibiotics, afebrilium, analgesics. Call his weight—let's see—ninety kilos. And make the dosage maximum."

Quarla nodded and hurried to the pharmacy room, while Snow bent back to the man. Even at this distance, Gann could see that the former Machine Colonel's face was contorted in agony and fear. There was more than sickness in Zafar's wild muttering; there was terror. He pushed himself erect, eyes staring, and shouted: "Graveyard of the galaxy! Starchild! Beware the trap! Beware your heart's desire!" Then Quarla was back with a spray hypodermic. Her father took it from her, pushed her out of the room again, and quickly injected the man.

Zafar slumped back onto the examining couch, eyes closing, still mumbling to himself.

The doctor watched him for a second, then came toward the group at the door. "He'll sleep for a while," he said. "Nothing else to do at this moment. We've got to see how he responds to the drug."

The man who had brought him said, "Doc, what is it? Are we all going to . . ." But Dr. Snow was shaking his head.

"I can't answer your question," he said. "I don't know what it is. But I don't think you're in any danger. I've seen only one other case like this, three years ago. But I was exposed, and so was my daughter, and several others—and no one was infected."

He hesitated, glancing at Gann. Then he said abruptly, "The other case was Harry Hickson, Mr. Gann. It killed him."

Boysie Gann started to speak, then nodded. "I understand."

"Do you?" Dr. Snow's voice was heavy with irony. "I don't! I don't understand at all. Let me show you something—then tell me if you understand!" He stood away from the door, reached out a hand, and switched off the lights in the emergency room. "Look!" he cried. "Do you understand that?"

The four in the doorway gasped as one. "Father!" cried Quarla, and the men swore softly. Inside the emergency room, in the semi-darkness Dr. Snow had brought about, Mohammed Zafar's leather-colored skin was leather-colored no longer. Like the spilled blood of the spaceling Gann had seen murdered, Zafar's skin was bright with a golden glow! His face shone with the radiance of a muted sun. One wasted hand, dangling out of the sheets, was limned in a yellowish, unsteady light like the flicker of a million flashing fusorians.

Quarla choked, "It's . . . it's just like Harry, Father!"

The doctor nodded somberly. "And it will end the same way, too. Unless there's a miracle, that man will be dead in an hour."

He sighed and reached to turn the light on again, but there was an abrupt hissing, swishing sound and something darted past them, over their heads. "What the devil!" cried Dr. Snow, and turned on the lights.

Something was on the dying man's head, something that scuttled about and glared at them with hot red eyes, like incandescent shoebuttons.

"Father! It's Harry's—I mean, it's the pyropod! The one Boysie and I brought back!" cried Quarla Snow.

Gann said tightly, "Look! He broke the chain." Then he laughed shakily. "Harry would be pleased," he said unsteadily. "At last the thing's learned how to fly."

Machine Colonel Zafar lived longer than the hour Dr. Snow had promised, but it was obvious that the extra time would not be very long. He was sinking. For minutes at a time he seemed hardly to breathe, then roused himself long enough to mumble incoherent phrases like "The Starchild! But the Swan won't help him . . ."

Snow was working over his laboratory equipment in the corner of the room, pausing every few minutes to check his patient's breathing, and shake his head. He summoned Quarla and Gann to him and gestured to a microscope.

"I want to show you something," he said, his face somber and wondering. "Look." And he stepped aside.

Quarla looked into the slim chromed barrels of the microscope, then lifted her head to stare questioningly at her father. He nodded. "You see? Mr. Gann, look."

Slowly Boysie Gann took her place. "I'm not a scientist, Doctor," he protested. "I won't know what to look for."

But then he was looking through the eyepieces and his voice stopped. He did not need to be a scientist. The spectacle before him, standing out clear in three dimensions in the stereoscopic field of the microscope, was nothing he had ever seen before.

Straw-colored erythrocytes and pale eosinophiles floated among colonies of benign microorganisms that live in every human's blood. Rodlike and amoeboid, radial or amorphous, all the tiny bacteria were familiar, in a vague, half-remembered way, to Gann.

All but one.

For dominating the field were masses of globular bodies, dark and uninteresting-looking at first, but bursting under his eyes into spurts of golden light. Like the luminous plankton of Earth's warm seas, they flared brilliantly, then subsided, then flared again. It was like tiny warning lights signaling disaster in the sample of the sick man's blood—hundreds of them, perhaps thousands—so many that the field of the microscope was brilliantly illuminated with a flickering golden glow.

"Great Plan!" whispered Boysie Gann. "And this is what made him sick?"

Dr. Snow said slowly, "It is the same thing I saw in Harry Hickson's blood. Just before he died."

He took his place at the twin eyepieces and glanced for a second at the tiny golden spheres. "Fusorians," he said. "It took me a month with paper chromatography and mass spectrograms to verify it in Harry's blood, but that is what they were. Colonies of fusorian symbiotes gone wild. They're killing him."

He stared blankly at the microscope, then roused himself and hurried back to his patient. Machine Colonel Zafar was gasping for breath, his eyes wide and fixed on the ceiling, his fingers working aimlessly, his whole skin suffused with that golden glow.

"Quarla!" rapped Dr. Snow. "Seal the room! We'll give him a positive partial pressure of oxygen! . . . It won't save his life," he added wearily, "but it may prolong it—by minutes, at least."

The girl hurried to close the door tightly against its resilient seals, while her father adjusted valves on his mediconsole. Boysie Gann heard a "white" sound of hissing gas and felt a quick increase of pressure in his ears.

He swallowed and heard Quarla's voice, queerly distant, say, "Father! He's—he's trying to get up!"

Machine Colonel Zafar was sitting up. His eyes were less remote, his breathing easier in the hypobaric atmosphere. But the golden glow was even more intense, the perspiration streaming from his brow.

And his eyes were on Boysie Gann. "You!" he cried. "Swan take you! Get back to the Machine, you traitor!" And he made the curious looping gesture with his arm that Gann had seen in Harry Hickson . . .

And then Boysie Gann remembered what the star was that lived in the heart of the Swan.

"Alpha Cygni!" he cried. "Deneb! The star in the constellation of the Swan!"

Zafar fell back on an elbow, glaring at him. "Your dirty mouth profanes the sacred name," he hissed. "The Starchild will punish you. In the heart of the Planner's citadel—in the bowels of Terra, where the Machine plays with its human toys—the Starchild will seek out and destroy its enemies!"

His eyes closed and he gasped for breath. Gann looked at Quarla and her father, but their expressions were as clouded as his own. "Starchild?" whispered the girl. "Father, do you know what—"

The doctor rumbled, "No, Quarla. I know nothing. Only rumors. A myth that there is a Starchild, and that he will bring the faithful of the Church of the Star home to Deneb's planets one day."

"No rumor!" shouted the glowing, golden man, and he paused to cough hackingly. "The Starchild lives! I've seen him in the heart of the Whirlpool! He has touched me with his radiant hand!"

But Dr. Snow was beside him, thrusting him back down on the bed, hushing him. "No!" cried Zafar wildly. "Don't stop the word of the Starchild! See here!"

And with a convulsive effort he drew out of the pouch

of the one garment he still wore a stiff, cream-colored sheet of parchment. "The Writ of Liberation!" he shouted. "The Starchild gave it to me to send to Earth. And I send it—now!"

The pyropod that had belonged to Harry Hickson scuttled wildly about, its red eyes bright orange in the high-oxygen air. It hissed and shook its scales; and Zafar's eyes, too, were almost orange, glowing with tiny, dancing golden atoms, even in the pupil. They seemed blind—or fixed on something far more distant than the walls of the doctor's clinic.

Boysie Gann felt a shudder, as if the floor of the room were shaking. It had not moved.

He staggered and thrust out a hand to support himself, yet there was no motion. "To Earth!" cried the sick man, and threw the sheet of paper from him. "Swan, carry it! Starchild, guide it! To Earth . . ." He broke off.

The doctor tried again to calm him, but the dying man thrust him aside. "To Earth!" he cried. "And you—spy, traitor, slave of the Machine! Swan take you . . ."

Gann opened his mouth to say something, anything, but words would not come. The room lurched again, more violently. Sickeningly. The others did not seem to notice, yet the shock came again. He stumbled and almost fell, caught himself and reached out instinctively for the fluttering sheet of paper Zafar had thrown into the air.

It slipped away from him . . . and disappeared. One moment it was there. The next moment it was gone. Where it had been Gann saw a queer flow in the atmosphere, like flawed glass, spinning.

The whirlpool grew. It enlarged and came near him, and the room moved around him once more. Frantically he tried to leap back, to save himself, but he was falling, falling into the whirlpool . . . falling . . . and falling . . .

He fell for what seemed to be a thousand years while

the room turned queerly dark and disappeared. Quarla's worried face, the doctor's look of shock, Mohammed Zafar's dying glare of hate—all disappeared, and around him he saw the dim shapes of stars and planets, of galaxies and dust clouds, rippling and glowing . . .

He fell for a long time, through what seemed to be a distance of billions upon billions of empty, airless miles.

And was.

For when the falling stopped and shaken and frantic he staggered to his feet, he fell flat and cut his face, bloodied his nose against a gray, soft-lighted metal floor.

He was in full Earth gravity.

He was on the Reefs no longer. He was on a planet. And around him stretched long empty corridors of metal walls and spinning tapes and glittering lights. Machine Major Boysie Gann was home at last. He was in the catacombs under Earth's surface that housed the mighty electronic masses of the Planning Machine.

VI

And that was how it began for Boysie Gann, with a
twenty-billion-mile drop that landed him in a place
where no one could possibly be, in the heart of the
Machine.

A warm wind blew between the narrow walls of the
corridor. There was a faint distant hum, overlaid by the
whir and hiss of rushing tape, the drone of enormous
far-off machines. Gann stood up, gasping with the effort of moving his new weight—nearly a hundred kilos,
when for months he had had to carry only a fraction
of that, or none. He looked around, dazed.

He was in a long corridor. At the end of it, hundreds
of yards off, was a brighter light that seemed to be a
room.

He stumbled toward it, stanching the flow from his
nose with the back of a hand, coughing and tasting the
acrid blood at the back of his mouth.

The gray light turned out to come from a strange
round chamber, its roof a high concrete dome. The great
floor was broken with little island clusters of consoles
and control panels, unattended. The wall, almost circular,
was pierced with twenty-four dark tunnels like the one
he had come from.

Gann leaned dizzily for a moment against the frame
of the door through which he had entered. Then, sum-

moning his strength, he shouted, "Help! Anyone! Is anybody here?"

The only answer was a booming echo from the great concrete dome, and the distant whirring of the tapes.

The control stations were empty, the corridor vacant. Yet as Gann stood there he began to feel that the place was somehow alive. As the echoes died away his ears began to register fainter, more distant sounds—a muffled mechanical murmur, a hum and whir. All the corridors were as empty as the one he had left. He peered into them one by one, saw nothing but the endless banks of computing equipment, the jungle of thick cables that roofed them.

Almost on tiptoes, humbled by the immense hush around him, Gann went to the circular islands of consoles in the middle of the chamber. One unit, glowing with illuminated dials and buttons, faced each radiating tunnel. He stood entranced, watching the race of indicator lights across the face of each console.

He had never seen this place in his own person before, yet it was all familiar to him, had been repeated a hundred times, from a hundred angles, in the texts and visual-aid lectures at the Technicorps academy. He was in the very heart of the Planning Machine—the most secret, the most elaborately guarded spot on nine planets. The nerve center of the Plan of Man.

And the Planning Machine did not even know he was there!

That was the fact that most shook Boysie Gann, almost terrified him, not only for himself, although surely he was on dangerous ground—men had gone to the Body Bank for far less. His fear was for the Plan of Man itself. How was it possible?

With all its storage of facts on every act of every human being in the Plan—with its great taped mass of data covering every field of knowledge, every scientific discovery, every law—the Planning Machine seemed to have no way of telling that an unauthorized human being was at large in its very heart.

Gann found himself sobbing. Dizzied, he clutched at the edge of the nearest console and frantically tried to make sense of the unfamiliar glitter of dials and scopes and racing lights. There was a linkbox! For a moment he was hopeful—yet the linkboxes to the Machine were meant only for those who had received communion, who wore the flat plate in their skulls that gave the Machine access to their cranial nerve centers. Dared he use the linkbox?

But what else was there? Gann thought swiftly, crazily, of punching a button at random—throwing a switch—turning a dial. Any small change would alert the Machine. Serving robots or human techs would be there in moments.

Then his eyes caught sight of a small, flat red plate, bearing a single bright-lit button, and one word. It was at the top of the console nearest him. The single word was STOP.

He stood staring at it for a long moment, forgetting to breathe. If that plate meant what it so clearly, unequivocally said, he had it in his power to . . . to . . .

To stop the Machine.

Machine Major Boysie Gann, Technicorps academy graduate, veteran of the spy school, trained and toughened against the worst a solar system could produce, found himself babbling in terrified hysteria. Stop the Machine! The thought was unbearable.

He flung himself on the linkbox, found a switch, wept, babbled, and sobbed into it. He was not speaking in the Mechanese that the Machine had developed for the links—didn't know it—would have forgotten it if he had known it. He was literally terrified, as nothing in his life had ever terrified him before.

When the squad of Plan Guardsmen in Machine gray came boiling out of the access elevators, racing down the corridors, their weapons at the ready, they found him slumped on the floor, all but unconscious.

Boysie Gann nearly died right then, with twenty bullets in his body. But the Techtenant in command issued a sharp order. He peered wonderingly at Gann, restrained his men, thought for a second, then shook his head. "Don't hurt him," he growled. "Or not so he can't talk! Let's get him up to the security office—fast!"

For four days Boysie Gann was questioned around the clock by the brawniest bullies in the Technicorps, and they were not gentle with him.

He answered all their questions—told the absolute truth—and paid for it with the impact of a club against his kidneys, a kick in his ribs. They knocked him unconscious a dozen times, and each time he revived again with a hard-faced medical orderly pulling a hypodermic out of his skin, brought back to face more interrogation.

Finally they let him sleep—not because they were satisfied with his answers, but because the medics feared he would die.

When he awoke he ached in every part of his body. He was strapped to an operating table. *The Body Bank*, he thought at first in a surge of panic. But it was not the Body Bank; it was a prison. Clearly the medics had been working on him. Although he ached, he could move. His toes curled, his fingers responded to his brain. His eyes opened and moved where he willed them.

Only one thing was different: there was a cold, hard pressure around his neck.

The security collar that Harry Hickson had removed so easily had been replaced.

Men were all around him, removing the straps, forcing him to his feet. "You! Risk," growled one of them, a radar-horned NCO with a chin that was stubbled blue with beard. "On your feet! You're going to talk to the general."

They hurried him through gray-walled corridors to an elevator. It rose with a sickening thrust of acceleration, stopped as rapidly. Gann nearly fell, but was thrust to his feet again by one of the guards. "Out! Move on, Risk!" And he stumbled through more corridors into a bare gray office, and there he stood at attention for a long, long time, waiting.

Then—Boysie Gann heard no signal, but perhaps it had been relayed through the radar-horned helmet of the guards—the security guardsman barked, "In there!" and thrust him through a door.

Gann entered a larger, brighter office. It was beautifully furnished, with a bust of the Planner in glowing gold smiling down from a pedestal, and a golden linkbox to the Machine dominating the desk. On the desk was a nameplate.

MACHINE GENERAL ABEL WHEELER

And the man who sat behind it was the general himself.

He sat regarding Boysie Gann for a long moment. Machine General Wheeler seemed more than half a machine himself. He was a big man, an angular, perplexing, abrupt-moving man. His whole body looked metallic: skin tan of bronze, eyes the color of steel, spikes of copper wire for hair. He stared at Gann and then, without a word, looked away, his eyes going to something invisible on his desk.

Boysie Gann felt choked by the hard, cold constriction of the security collar. Bruises aching, skin clammy with sweat, he stood painfully rigid. At the Technicorps academy he had learned the art of standing endlessly at attention—the imperceptibly slow shifting of weight and muscular tensions that kept a man from pitching forward on his face. He blanked out his mind, thought of nothing but of the importance of standing there.

The general's frowning eyes clung to the tilted communications screens that faced him on his desk, invisible to Gann. After a moment he tapped soundless keys, communicating, Gann knew, with the Machine. Gann wondered that he did not use the linkbox. It did not occur to him that the general might fear that Boysie Gann, the man who had appeared inexplicably in the heart of the Planning Machine's caverns, might equally inexplicably have learned to understand Mechanese.

The general waited, reading something, frowning stiffly. Abruptly his head jerked up and he stared at Gann.

The screens had ceased to flicker. His flat bronzed face was expressionless. It was a mask of meat, as if some bungling surgeon at the replacement center had failed to connect the nerves and muscles that would have given it life.

General Wheeler said sharply, "Machine Major Boysie Gann!" Gann jumped; he could not help himself; the voice was like a metal rasp. "You may stand at ease!"

Gann let his lean shoulders sag slightly forward, drew a long breath, shifted his feet. But he was not really at ease. General Wheeler's eyes were on him, steel-colored, as coldly merciless as if they were the probes of a surgeon planting electrodes in his brain. He snapped, "The Machine requires information from you."

Gann said painfully, "I know, sir. I've already been interrogated—about a hundred times, I'd say."

"It will be a thousand! You will be interrogated again and again and again. The Machine's need for truth is urgent." Wheeler's broad head jutted forward like the sudden thrust of a piston. "The Starchild! Who is he?"

There was a dry lump in Gann's throat. He swallowed and said stubbornly, "I don't know, sir. I've told everything I know."

"The Writ of Liberation! Who wrote it?" Gann shook his head. "How did it get into the Planner's headquarters?" Gann kept on shaking his head, hopelessly but obstinately. "And yourself, how did you get into the Planning Machine's tunnels? Who is Quarla Snow? Why did you kill Machine Colonel Zafar and make up this preposterous lie?"

"No, sir!" cried Gann. "I didn't! Colonel Zafar was anti-Plan!"

The general's wide mounth hardened. His bloodless lips shut like the jaws of a trap. His voice was like a muffled, ominous clang. "The evidence," he said, "suggests that you are lying. Can you prove you are not?"

"No, sir. But—"

"Machine Mayor Boysie Gann! Are *you* the Starchild?"

"No, sir!" Gann was honestly surprised, indignant. "I—"

"Machine Major Boysie Gann! Do you know what became of the *Togethership?*"

Gann cried hopelessy: "The what? General, I never even heard of the—what is it? The *Togethership.* I don't know what you're talking about."

Like the steady pulse of a laser scan, the general tolled: "The *Togethership* went into space forty years ago. It was never heard of again. Major Gann, what do you know of this?"

"Nothing, sir! Why, I wasn't even born!"

For a moment the mask cracked, and the general's face looked almost human. Worried. Even confused. He said after a moment, "Yes. That's true. But . . ."

Then he tightened up again, bent forward stiffly from the hips. His steel eyes narrowed. "Are you loyal to the Plan of Man?" he asked softly.

"Yes, sir!"

The general nodded. "I hope so," he said bleakly. "For the sake of the Plan—and for your own sake, too. For I am going to tell you something that cannot ever be told again. If you whisper a word of it, Machine Major Boysie Gann, your death will come at once. *At once.*

"You see, the Planning Machine is not unique. There is another one."

Gann's eyes widened. "Another . . ." he stopped, and had to begin again. It was like being told there were two Jehovahs, a second Christ. "Another Planning Machine, sir? But where is it?"

The general shook his head. "Lost," he said somberly. "Another Machine—as great, as powerful, as complete as the one that guides the Plan of Man. And we do not know where it is.

"Or what it is doing."

There was a man name Ryeland, the general told Boysie Gann. A great mathematician. A brilliant scientist. The husband of the daughter of the then-Planner, and close to the center of power surrounding the Planning Machine itself. And decades before he had gone into space, just as Gann himself had done, and seen the Reefs of Space, and come back with the tale of countless thousands of unplanned humans living their lives out on the fusorian worldlets, outside the scope of the Plan.

"What he said," rasped General Wheeler sternly, "was false! But the Machine wisely determined to test it out! The Planning Machine does not leap to conclusions! It weighs the evidence—learns the facts—makes a plan!"

"Yes, sir," said Boysie Gann. "I've heard of this Ryeland, I think. A leading scientist even today!"

The general nodded. "Today," he said cryptically, "Ryeland has abandoned error. A loyal servant of the Plan. And so is the former Planner, Creery, who also has turned away from falsity. But then . . ." He sighed, like the wheezing of a high-vacuum pump.

Then, he told Gann, both men had been duped—and had caused the Machine to commit . . . not an error, of course—that was impossible to the Machine—but to conduct an experiment that failed.

The experiment was to bring the Plan of Man to the Reefs.

The Machine had directed the construction of a mighty spacecraft called the *Togethership*. The biggest space-going vessel ever built, a mobile spacefort, it was fabricated at the yards on Deimos, and powered with six detachable jetless drive units that were themselves great fighting ships. And more than half of its hull was filled with a slave unit of the Planning Machine—a linked bank of computers and storage banks, as advanced as the Machine itself, lacking only the network of communications and implementation facilities that the Machine had developed out of the race of Man.

The *Togethership* was built, launched, tested, and fitted out. A selected crew was assembled and came aboard. Supplies were loaded for a ten-year cruise. The slave Machine assumed control . . . the *Togethership* flashed out past Orbit Pluto—passed the Spacewall—and was gone.

Days later a message came back via laser relay chain. All was going well. The *Togethership* had sighted a major cluster of the Reefs of Space.

No other message was ever received.

Machine General Wheeler paused, his steel-gray eyes on Gann. "No other message," he repeated. "It has never been heard from again. Scouting vessels, attempting to locate it, came back without having found any trace. Or did not come back at all. Or returned early, damaged, having been attacked by pyropods or something worse.

"That is the story of the *Togethership*, Major Gann. Except for one thing: the cluster of Reefs it last reported sighting was in the same position as what you have called Freehaven. And you were there, Major. What did you learn?"

Wonderingly, Gann shook his head. "Nothing, sir. Believe me. Not even a rumor."

The general looked at him for a long second. Then he nodded. "Gann," he said bleakly, "I will tell you one more thing." Abruptly he snapped three switches on his desk, glanced at a monitoring dial, nodded. "We are cut off," he declared. "Not even the Planning Machine can look in on us now. What I have to tell you is for *no* ears but your own.

"You see, Gann, it is not only the welfare of the Plan of Man that is involved here. I have a special interest in solving these mysteries. Solving them myself.

"Major Gann, I intend to be the next Planner."

Boysie Gann was adrift in dangerous waters, and he knew it. He had heard rumors of the power struggle of the human leaders who surrounded the great central power-fact of the Machine, jockeying for position, seeking personal advantage. The Technicorps Academy had been filled with sly jokes and blazing-eyed, after-dark discussions of it. Some had viewed the political strife as treason (though they dared only whisper the thought). Some had taken it as a joke, or as a natural law of human affairs which they proposed to follow for their own advancement. Gann remembered the brother of the girl he had left at Playa Blanca, a white-hot idealist—

remembered one of his instructors, a cynical humorist whose japes had seemed half in earnest and had set his classes wriggling with astonishment and something like fear. The instructor had disappeared one day. The young cadet who was Julie Martinet's brother had become an honor student at the academy. He had even gone on to spy school on Pluto, just as Gann himself was leaving.

But idealist or cynic, whatever the attitude of the individual, the whole question of political maneuvering had been remote. It was something that took place far off, high up—not in the life of Boysie Gann.

Not until now.

Machine General Abel Wheeler leaned forward from his desk and rapped out the words: "I must know this. Do you know who sent the Writ of Liberation?"

Gann shook his head. "Sir, I've never even seen it. I don't know what it says."

"Foolish threats, Major Gann! An insane promise to stop the sun's light. A warning to the Planner and to the Machine that freedom must be restored—hah! And yet" —the man's steel eyes grew colder and more distant still, as he contemplated something far away—"it seems that there is something behind the threats. For the sun is indeed stopped."

He paused. Boysie Gann blinked. "Stopped? The sun? Sir, I don't understand . . ."

"Nor do I," rasped the general, "but that does not matter. What matters is the security of the Machine. It matters particularly to me, since I am entrusted with its defense. This Writ of Liberation is a threat; I must protect the Machine against it. If I am successful, I will receive . . . a suitable reward. To those who can help me . . ." He glanced about his spy-tight room, leaned farther forward still, and merely mouthed the words: "I can offer them rewards, too, Major Gann."

His steel eyes stabbed restlessly about the room, then returned to Gann. "Major," he said. "I need you for a friend."

Gann was still turning over in his mind what the general had said about the stoppage of the sun. The sun? No longer shining in the sky? It was hard to believe. He shook himself free from the questions that were burning at him and said uneasily, "I hope to be your friend, sir. But I still know nothing of the Starchild!"

The general nodded like a metronome. "You will be questioned again," he rapped out. "This time, directly by the Machine, through one of its servitors—a human who has taken the Machine's communion and speaks directly to it. This will perhaps help you to remember certain things. It may even be that from the questions the acolyte asks, you may be able to deduce other things— perhaps even make a guess at things that are stored in the memory banks of the Machine that even I do not know. If so," he said, his face a bronze mask, "I will be interested. The choice is yours. My friend or my foe— and even now," he added, his bronze jaws hardening, "I have power enough to punish my foes."

He opened the switches again, glanced at his communications screens, nodded, tapped out an answer, and turned once more to Gann.

"You will go now to Sister Delta Four," he stated. "There your direct link questioning to the Machine will begin. Major, look at this!"

Unexpectedly he raised his right fist. It clenched like a remote manipulator into a bronze hammer. "This hand," he droned somberly, "once belonged to someone else, an unplanned traitor who threw a bomb at the Planner. His aim was poor. He missed the Planner but his bomb shattered my own right hand.

"My hand could not be repaired by the surgeons, so

it was replaced. With the hand of the would-be assassin."
The bronze fist slammed against the console.

"Gann, remember this! If you fail to serve the Machine in the way that is first required, you will serve it in some other way—more than likely in the Body Bank!"

VII

The radar-horned guards were waiting.

"Come on, Risk!" growled the NCO in charge, and once again Boysie Gann was thrust and dragged through the long gray halls, into the elevators, out again—and left to wait in a bare gray room.

Only for a moment. Then the guards came back, looking angry and confused. "Come on, Risk!" growled the NCO again—he seemed to know no other words, be able to speak in no other way—and Gann was taken out again.

A girl was standing in the doorway, telling her sonic beads, her head bent. She wore the robe and cowl of one of the Machine's communing acolytes, one of those adepts who had learned the Mechanese that the Machine now spoke in preference to any other language, whose very brain centers were open to the touch of the Machine. As they passed she spoke to one of the guards. "Orders changed!" he said roughly. "Come along if you like—we're going to the Planner!"

Gann hung back, trying to turn and see her, but the NCO shoved him ahead. He could hear the girl's oddly melodious voice, not so much speaking as chanting Mechanese in the quarter tones of her sonic beads, but could not make out her words.

She would be—what had General Wheeler called her? Sister Delta Four. The one who was to interrogate him.

But he was going instead to the office of the Planner himself!

In all his years of life under the Plan, Boysie Gann had never seen the Planner in the flesh. Few had. There was no need, with communications reaching into every home, even every room under the Plan—and the Planner was something more than human, removed from even the condescending social intercourse of emperors.

Gann shivered slightly. He was already assuming the attitudes of the convict of any land or time. He feared change. He dreaded the unknown. And the Planner rep-represented a very large unknown quantity indeed.

Again the tunnels, again the high-velocity drop of the elevators. Again Gann was thrust into a tiny room and left there.

He was somewhere far underground. Listening, he could hear no sound except the muffled murmur of air from the duct overhead. The walls were an unpleasant yellowish gray—no longer quite the sterile Technicorps color, but tinged with Planner's gold. Gann wondered if it was deliberate, or if it was merely that this cell was so old, its occupants viewed with so little favor, that the baked-in coloring of the walls had yellowed with age. The ceiling gave a cold gray light. There was only one bare metal table and one bare metal chair.

The security collar was hard against his throat.

Gann sat down and laid his head on the table. His bruises were beginning to stiffen and ache. His brain was whirling.

Confused images were filling his mind. General Wheeler and his menacing hints of reward. Quarla Snow's spaceling, and the pyropods. Julie Martinet. A daytime sky with the sun somehow gone out . . . the sunlike fusorian globules in Colonel Zafar's blood . . . Julie Martinet again, and Quarla Snow.

He lived again the endless frightening drop that landed him in the bowels of the planet Earth, among the memory banks of the Machine. He saw again sterile Pluto's vistas of ice, and the great slow spin of Polaris Station. He thought of the Writ of Liberation and wondered at the love for freedom of the Planless men of the Reefs—the love for freedom—the freedom to love . . .

He thought again of Julie Martinet, and submerged himself in memories of the Togetherness resort at Playa Blanca, the slight, dark girl he had heard singing, their golden dawn together on the beach, with the taste of salt spray on her lips. He could see her face as clearly as if she were in the room with him.

"Julie," he whispered, and she opened her lips to reply . . .

"Come on, Risk!" she said queerly—roughly. "Get up! Move!"

The radar-horned NCO was shaking him angrily. "Risk! Wake up!"

Gann shook himself. He had been asleep. His arm was numb and tingling where his head had rested on it.

He was still dazed as they dragged him out of the cell, into another room—larger, brighter, furnished in splendor. It was all gold. Gold tapestries on the wall, showing the spinning worlds of the Plan of Man. Gold light fixtures, and gold trays on the golden tables. The floor a carpeting of gold, the furniture upholstered in a golden fabric.

A guard stood by him at each side, gripping his arms. They brought him to the center of the room and stood there, waiting, while the NCO went to a gold-arched door and whispered to a Technicorps officer in the uniform of the Planner's guard who stood there. The officer nodded impatiently and held up a hand.

The radar-horned guard turned and signaled to his men. *Wait.*

Boysie Gann was very sure, without being told, of where they were. Beyond that door was the Planner himself.

They were not alone in the room. Turning his neck —the grip of the guards did not allow him to turn his body—he saw that the acolyte girl, Sister Delta Four, was in the room, kneeling on a golden hassock, telling her sonic beads. She was slight. What small sight he could get of her face, under the great soft cowl, was oval, grave, and pale. Her loose black robe fell to the floor around the hassock. Her cape bore the luminous emblem of those who had undergone communion with the Machine—the symbolic ellipses of electronic orbits intertwined.

The guards wrenched him straight again. One whispered to the other across him, "Watch! She's going to go into communion."

Even in his precarious position Gann could not help wanting to see. He had never before been with an acolyte during communion. It was something to be desired—and dreaded.

If the deadly security collar around his neck was the stick that the Machine had invented to enforce the Plan of Man, the communion plate was the carrot that rewarded faithful service.

Gann knew what it looked like. He thought he had caught a glimpse of it in the forehead of Sister Delta Four, the bright metal disk grafted into the skin, starred with its black pattern of holes that accepted the prongs of the communion plug.

He knew that communion was supposed to be the perfect experience. The communion plate was only its exterior symbol. It was in the brain itself that the delicate stereotaxia of the Machine's neurosurgeons had done their finest work. Through electrodes wired to the plate in the forehead, the Machine requited its deserving servants with tuned electronic stimuli. It messages flowed directly into the pleasure centers of the brain.

The perfect experience—for it had no taint of reality to corrupt it, no bill presented in the form of exhaustion or physical damage—no substance! It was the quintessence of pleasure. Stripped of tactile, visual, olfactory—of all sensual complications—it was the great good thing that men had always sought, and found imperfectly as a side effect of eating, or drinking, or inhaling the crisp air of a mountain morning, or sex. It was all of them, distilled and served up in a tidy package, received through a bright metal plate.

It was so perfect, thought Boysie Gann wildly, that it seemed somehow wrong . . .

"She's getting ready!" whispered one of the guards, and Gann ventured to turn his head again to see.

He succeeded—only for a moment, but he succeeded. The guards were watching too, and loosened their grips just enough for him to turn.

Sister Delta Four lifted the black hood to uncover her forehead. There on the smooth white skin he saw the bright metal disk—saw it, trembled, looked away—looked back again, and saw clearly what his mind had rejected.

He saw the face of Sister Delta Four.

There was a hoarse whisper from the doorway. "Let's go!" The guards started, and jerked him away, thrust him facing forward so that he saw the radar-horned NCO with a face like fury, beckoning them angrily, signaling that the Planner was ready for them now.

But Boysie Gann fought them, struggled like a wild man. "No!" he shouted. "Wait!" And he battled the astonished guards, trying to turn, to go back to the girl whose serene face he had seen, eyes closed, lifting the communion plug to her forehead.

The guards lashed out at him, struck him. He hardly felt the blows. He turned, breaking free of one of them, colliding heavily with the other so that they fell sprawling on the thick golden rug, the other guards leaping toward them. But as they fell, Gann saw the face again.

He had been right. There was no doubt. Sister Delta Four was Julie Martinet.

The girl he loved was now no longer entirely human. Her vows were no longer to him. She was an adjunct to the Machine, as dependent on it for her every bit of life and thought as some remote-directed subsea mining dredge . . . and as little a part of the race of men.

Julie Martinet had become a part of the machine.

VIII

If the catacombs of the Machine were the nerve center of the Plan of Man, then the great State Hall of the Planner was its heart. Huge as a hangar for jetless spacecraft, ornate as a Pharaoh's tomb, it housed the most powerful man in the history of the human race, and it was worthy of him. The walls were paneled in gold. Crescent-shaped lunettes were frescoed with scenes of the nine planets and a thousand lesser worlds on which the Plan of Man reigned supreme.

In the great hall, a score of attendants waited on the Planner's will: his personal physician, three black-robed Mechanese acolytes with their linkboxes and tonal beads, a dozen guards. The Vice-Planner for Venus was there, an efficient little engineer whose nose and ears were out of scale, seeming to have come from some gigantic donor. So was Machine General Wheeler, fixing Boysie Gann as he entered with a steel-gray stare.

No one spoke.

Dominating the great hall, on a huge golden chair, was the Planner himself. He was staring, lost in thought, at a great quartz table on which stood scores of fantastic metal and crystal toys.

Gann found himself standing in the center of a great tesselated floor, alone. His guards had halted behind him. He waited for the Planner to notice him.

But the Planner's eyes were on his toys. He sighed and stretched out a hand to them, stacking them in military rows as absorbedly as any five-year-old with his lead soldiers; he formed them in columns and marched them across the clean gleaming quartz.

The figures were dragons. They were monsters from storybooks, and creatures too incredible ever to have been in a story. Some were mirror-bright, some black. Many were in gorgeous rainbow hues. They had no wings, nor had they legs. Their heads were the heads of monsters, some with teeth like sabers, some with curious frayed flower-petal faces, like the muzzle of a star-nosed mole.

Boysie Gann had never been close to the Planner before. He could not help being a little disappointed. The Planner was only a man! An old, fat, flabby man at that —and, thought Gann privately, a bit of an eccentric too.

Yet the Planner was the voice of the Planning Machine itself. It was impossible for the Machine to falter in its judgments, impossible that its chosen instrument be anything less than perfect. Of course, there were the recurrent rumors about the present Planner's predecessors —old Planner Creery, for example, who had fallen into error in attempting to allow the Reefs of Space entry into the Plan of Man under their own conditions . . . Swiftly Gann rejected that thought. This was no place to be thinking treason!

He turned his mind to the stabbing pain that had pierced him in the anteroom when he had found the girl he loved, Julie Martinet, changed into a priestess of the Machine, Delta Four. How had it happened? *Why* had it happened? . . .

The Planner raised his great round head and stared at Boysie Gann. "You," he rasped. "Do you know what these are?"

Gann swallowed and stuttered. "Y-yes, sir," he got out.

"I mean, I think so. I mean, some of them look like pyropods. The creatures that prey on the life in the Reefs of Space, sir . . ."

But the Planner was nodding his great bloated head. "Pyropods, yes," he boomed. With a sudden motion he swept the delicately carved pieces off the quartz table, sent them crashing to the floor. "I wish I had a thousand pyropods!" he shouted. "A million! I wish I could send them out to the Reefs to kill and destroy every living thing on them! What insanity that these reef rats should dare talk to me of freedom!"

He broke off and glared at Boysie Gann, who stood silent, unable to speak. The Planner said, "I stand for classic truth! What is it that animates the Reefs of Space, Gann? Tell me, for you have been there. It is the romantic fallacy," he roared, not waiting for an answer, "the eternal delusion that man is perfectible, that there is a spirit of goodness that can grow and mature in crass organic creatures! What insanity! And now they threaten me in my own Hall—blot out my sun—boast of more deadly measures still!" He pressed his plump arms against the carved golden arms of his chair, half lifted himself, leaned forward to Gann and shouted, "Who is this Starchild, Gann? It is you?"

Boysie Gann was galvanized into shocked speech. "No, sir! Not me! I've never seen him. I know nothing about him—oh, except what I've heard here, when General Wheeler's men interrogated me. And a few rumors. But I'm not the Starchild!"

"Rumors. What are those rumors, Gann? I must know!"

Gann looked helplessly around the great hall. All in it were watching him, their eyes cold, their faces impassive. He was on his own; there was no help for him from anyone there. He said desperately, "Sir, I've told all I know a hundred times. I'll tell it again. I'll tell you all I know, but the truth is, sir, that I know almost nothing about the Starchild!"

"The truth," boomed the Planner, "is what *I* say it is! Go on! Speak!"

Gann obediently commenced the old story. "I was detailed, sir, to investigate certain irregularities on Polaris Station . . . ." As he went through the long, familiar tale there was dead silence in the hall, the Planner listening impassively, leaning on one arm in his great golden chair, the others taking their cue from him. Gann's voice fell on the enormous hall like words shouted down a well. Only echoes answered him, only the narrowing of an eye, the faint shift of a position showed that his hearers had understood. He finished with his arrest in the catacombs of the Machine, and stood silent.

The Planner said thoughtfully, "You spoke of a sign. The sign of the Swan."

"Yes, sir." Boysie Gann demonstrated as best he could the supple motion of forearm and hand that he had seen in Harry Hickson and the dying Colonel Zafar. "I believe it refers to the constellation Cygnus, in which the main star, Deneb, is some sort of object of worship to what is called the Church of the Star . . ."

The Planner turned his great head away from Gann toward the black-robed knot of communicants of the Machine. "Deneb!" he barked. "Display it!" One of the acolytes spoke in soft, chiming tones to his linkbox. Instantly the lights in the great hall darkened, and on the vaulted ceiling a panorama sprang into light. The Planner craned his thick neck to stare searchingly upward. Every eye followed his.

It was as if the thousand yards of earth and rock above them had rolled back. They were gazing into the depths of space on what seemed to be a clear, moonless night—late in autumn, Gann judged by the position of the constellations; perhaps around midnight. Overhead were the great bright stars of the Summer Triangle, Altair to the south, Deneb and Vega to the north. The Milky Way banded the vault with a great irregular powder of stardust. Low on the horizon to the west red Antares glowed; to the east was Fomalhaut. . .

Abruptly the scene began to contract. It was as if they were rushing through space, straight toward the constellation Cygnus. Fomalhaut and Antares slipped out of sight with Sagittarius and Altair's constellation, the Eagle; so did the Pole Star and Cepheus below it; all that was left was Cygnus, the constellation of the Swan, hanging over their heads like a bright canopy.

A voice chimed, "Constellation Cygnus. Stars: Alpha Cygni, also known as Deneb, blue-white, first magnitude. Beta Cygni, also known as Albireo, double, components deep blue and orange. Gamma Cygni—"

The Planner's voice cut it in raspingly: "Just Deneb, idiot! What about Deneb?"

The voice did not miss a beat. It chimed: "Deneb, distance four hundred light-years. Surface temperature eleven thousand degrees. Supergiant. Spectrographic composition, hydrogen, calcium—"

"Planets!" boomed the Planner irritably.

"No planets known," sang the invisible voice. Gann craned his neck; it came from one of the black-robed acolytes, but with their faces shrouded in the hoods he could not tell which.

The Planner was silent for a long time, staring upward. He said at last, "Has the Machine any evidence of physical connection between Deneb and the Starchild?"

"No evidence, sir," chanted the invisible voice at once. "Exceptions as follows: Possible connection between star Deneb and reported Church of the Star. Possible connection between star Deneb and star 61 Cygni in same constellation, 61 Cygni being one of the stars said Starchild threatened to, and did, extinguish. Neither of these items considered significant by the Machine."

The Planner grumbled. "Very well. Cancel." The display overhead winked out, the room lights sprang up. The Planner sat brooding for a moment, his eyes remote. He stared absently around the room, his gaze passing over Boysie Gann, over the spilled toys at his feet, over the faces of the guardsmen and Machine General Wheeler.

His eyes came to rest on the black-robed acolytes. Then he sighed and gestured to one of them. It was only the crook of a finger, but the figure in black at once came toward him, holding something in his hand. It was a length of golden cable extending from his linkbox. At its end was a golden eight-pronged plug.

Boysie Gann's eyes went wide.

If he was not insane—and no, he was not; for already the acolyte was stepping to the Planner's side, touching his forehead, sweeping back his sparse, unruly hair, baring the glittering plate that was set into his forehead—the Planner was about to undergo communion with the Machine!

The spectacle was fascinating—and frightening.

Heedless of the eyes on him, the Planner sat relaxed while the acolyte deftly slipped the golden plug into the receptors in the plate on his forehead.

At once the Planner's expression changed. His eyes closed. The fretful, angry look disappeared. There was a second's grimace, the teeth bared in rictus, the corners of the eyes wrinkling in deep furrows, the jaw set. It was like a momentary pang of agony . . . Or ecstasy.

It passed, and the Planner's face went blank again. His breathing began to grow more rapid. As the planted electrodes excited the secret centers of his brain, he began to show feeling. His face creased in a smile, then frowned, then smiled again, forgivingly. His lips began to move. Hoarse, inarticulate words whispered—slowly . . . then faster, faster. His plump body shook, his fingers worked. The black-robed acolyte calmly touched his arm, whispered in his ear.

The Planner calmed. His body relaxed again. His whispered voice stopped.

The acolyte waited for a second, nodded, removed the cable and stepped lightly away. The Planner opened his eyes and looked around.

To Boysie Gann, the change in the Planner was stranger than anything he had seen on the Reefs of Space. A glum, angry, harried man had accepted that moment of communication with the electronic joys of the Machine; a cheerful, energetic, buoyant one had emerged from it. The Planner opened his mouth and boomed laughter into the great hall. "Ha!" he shouted. "Ho! That's good!"

He sat up and pounded his great fist onto the quartz table. "We'll destroy them!" he cried. "Reef rats and Starchild—anyone who dares interfere with the Plan of Man. We'll crush them and their fanciful dreams forever. And you'll help in this, Boysie Gann, for you are the chosen instrument of the Plan in this great work!"

For a lunatic moment Gann thought of turning, running, fleeing—of leaping toward the Planner and letting the decapitation charge in his security collar end his problems forever. There was something wild and fearful in the great chuckling good humor with which the Planner bubbled now, something that terrified Gann. If the Machine could cause such personality change in its most favored of servants, Gann feared the Machine. Feared it! And that thought was in itself fearsome to him, for the Machine had always been the great good master whose judgments were infallible, who always rewarded good service, punished only the bad. Yet this particular reward seemed a very terrible punishment to Gann . . .

But all he said was "Yes, sir. I serve the Plan, sir!"

The Planner shouted with glee. "Serve it well, boy!" he cried. "Serve it with all your heart and mind—or you'll serve it with your eyes and arms and liver, in the Body Bank! We all serve the Plan, boy. In one way or another!" And he dismissed Gann with a good-humored wave of one fat arm and turned to General Wheeler. As the guards closed in on Gann and marched him out of the room he caught one glimpse of the general, staring toward him. The steel-gray eyes were cold and empty, but Gann could read their message.

Don't fail me, either, Gann, they said.

IX

There had once been a time, thought Boysie Gann, when life was simple and his duty clear. In that dead, half-forgotten time—was it only months ago? it seemed like centuries—he had found, and loved, and won a girl named Julie Martinet. He remembered the night they met, remembered their long hours together, their endless promises, the bright hope of happiness they gave each other. He remembered the long white beach at the Togetherness center at Playa Blanca, and her kiss before he left. Warm, sweet, soft, loving, she had been everything a man could want. Her memory had followed Boysie Gann twenty billion miles out from the sun, and her absence had made that long voyage bleak.

Yet never had he been so far from her as in this room. He could, if he dared, reach out and touch the lips he had kissed at Playa Blanca. But the mind behind them was no longer the mind of the sweet, warm girl he had loved. The body was the body of Julie Martinet, but what inhabited it was Sister Delta Four.

Involuntarily he whispered: "Julie! Julie Martinet..."

She stood motionless, regarding him with grave dark eyes. He searched them for some hint of recognition, for the saving warmth of love that had filled them at Playa Blanca, but nothing was there.

She shook her hooded head. "I am Delta Four," she

said, her voice a melodious chime. "I am to interrogate you for the Machine." She stood watching him, waiting for a response, her pale face half hidden by the deep folds of the cowl she wore. The luminous emblem on her black robes mocked him. It was a *Keep Off* sign that he dared not ignore.

But he could not help saying, "Julie, don't you remember me at all? Can't you tell me what happened?"

She fingered her long string of bright black beads, each an electronic bell that rang when she stroked it. "Major Gann," she sang, her voice in perfect pitch with the tonal beads, "I am, as you see, an acolyte of the Machine. I do not wish to be reminded of any other life."

"Please, Julie. At least tell me why you didn't wait—"

Her grave head nodded. "We have time," she trilled. "Ask your question."

"Why didn't you—I mean, why didn't Julie Martinet wait for me? I sent you a letter from Pluto—"

"Your message was delivered," she sang. "But Julie Martinet had already been admitted to training as acolyte for the Machine. She destroyed your message. She does not wish to recall it."

"But I loved you!" Gann burst out. "How could you turn your back on me?"

The serene pale face stared at him without curiosity. "Julie Martinet loved you," she corrected him melodiously. "I am Delta Four. Please sit down, Major Gann. I must interrogate you for the Machine."

Reluctantly Gann sank into a chair, watched as she moved another chair near his. She seated herself with deliberate grace.

From under the cape she brought forth a small linkbox, covered in a black plastic, like leather. "Major Gann," she said, "I must ask you if you are the Starchild." Her voice was pure melody, cold and perfect and remote as her white, oval face.

Gann snapped, "Plan take it, no! I'm fed up with that question! I've said it a hundred—"

But she was shaking her head. "Wait," she broke in. "One moment, please."

He watched her glumly, the ache of his bruises combining with the deeper ache in his heart as, hooded head intently bent, she once again touched the long string of beads. As each electronic chime rang out her throat echoed the tone, practicing the difficult scale of tone phonemes that made up the artificial language called Mechanese.

Mechanese was the difficult bridge between the Machine and the human mind. Earlier computers had crossed that bridge by building their own structure of translation, transforming English into Fortran or another artificial tongue, Fortran into binary numbers, the binary statement into instructions and data for processing. The Machine's language was itself a sort of pattern of binary digits that represented its own electronic processes—circuits open or closed, storage points charged or discharged, ferrite cores in one magnetic state or another.

Human beings could not be trained to speak that binary language, nor could the Machine of the Plan of Man be troubled with the dull task of translation. Instead, it had created a language that men could learn—with difficulty, with a consecration of purpose that required them to give up the coarser human aspects of their lives, but all the same with accuracy and assurance.

Mechanese was a bridge, but a difficult one. The Machine, counting time in nanoseconds, could not wait for laggard human speech. Accurate in every either-or response, it had no need of redundancy. It had computed the theoretical capacity of the human ear and the human voice at some 50,000 binary units of information per second, and it had devised a tongue to approach that theoretical maximum.

Normal human speech conveyed only about fifty such bits of information in a second; Mechanese was a thousand times more efficient.

And, Gann knew, it was about a thousand times as difficult to learn.

Bitterly he realized that it was the very thing in Julie Martinet that first drew his attention to her—her soft, true voice—that had lost her for him forever. The Machine sought endlessly for humans who could be trained to Mechanese—sought them and, when it found them, did not let them go. Only such special individuals could be trained to speak Mechanese well, though it was possible for almost anyone who invested the time and effort to learn a sort of pidgin, or to understand it. A true acolyte needed not only a wide vocal range but a true sense of absolute pitch. The tonal beads would help. An acolyte could, as Delta Four was doing now, use them as a sort of pitch pipe before talking to the Machine. But not even they would convert an ordinary human into one fluent in Mechanese.

Watching her tolling the tonal beads, Gann pictured the long, arduous weeks of training. He knew it required total concentration, absolute devotion. And its ultimate reward was the bright metal plate in her forehead.

Her quick voice trilled a chain of silver bird notes. The linkbox sang an electronic answer. Her alert, emotionless eyes looked up at him at last.

"We're ready now," she said. "Major Gann. Are you the Starchild?"

A hundred interrogations, and this was the hundred and first.

Boysie Gann no longer needed his mind to answer the girl's questions. Repetition had taught his tongue and lips to answer by themselves. I am not the Starchild. I have never seen the Starchild. I know nothing of the Writ of Liberation. I have never engaged in unplanned activities.

And all the time his heart was shouting: *Julie! Come back . . .*

Each time he answered a question, Sister Delta Four sang into the linkbox. The strange, quavering notes sounded nothing like what he had said, but he knew that each difficult phoneme was also a meaningful morpheme, each sung syllable a clause. And each time she asked a question she paused, regarding him with detached interest, her perfect face as inhuman as her voice.

"My tour of hazardous duty took me out to the Spacewall . . ." he said, and went on with the long familiar tale.

He felt the bright gold walls pressing in on him, suddenly suffocating. He wondered how many thousand feet of rock lay above him. Up at the surface of the earth, was the endangered sun shining now on woods and fields tinted faintly green with early spring? Or was there arctic ice above this isolated, sound-deadened cell in the Planner's vast suites? Or miles, perhaps, of dark and icy ocean?

He had no way of knowing.

And abruptly he felt a wave of desperate longing for the Reefs, for Freehaven, for Quarla Snow. Those strange spaceborne rocks were somehow kinder than the Plan of Man. He was homesick for infinite space . . . for that fantastic concept freedom . . .

The stern snarl of the linkbox brought him back to his interrogation. "Proceed," cooed Sister Delta Four. "You were attacked by pyropods?" Her voice was as tuneful as a crystal bell, cold and empty as the black space between the Reefs. There was no flicker of feeling on the serene and secret oval of her face.

He nodded wearily—then, remembering: "Yes, but before that, I forgot to mention one thing. Hickson removed my collar."

Her brilliant dark eyes did not widen. She merely sang into the linkbox, still watching him, her eyes intent but somehow blind, as if she were already absorbed in her private ecstasy of communion.

The black box snarled.

"The Machine requires elucidation," Sister Delta Four trilled sweetly. "We must find this unregimented Harry Hickson. His knowledge must be recovered for the Plan. Then each organ of his body must be obliterated."

Gann grinned bleakly at her, looking at the lips he had kissed so long ago. "Sorry. I can't help you. He's dead."

"The Machine rejects this data," she sang. "Did you not ask this unplanned man how he removed the collar?"

"I don't know how," he admitted. He paused, hoping to see some living spark in her eyes. But there was none. The black box whirred ominously. "I think he was a convert to the Church of the Star," said Gann hurriedly. "I think—that is, as I understand it, his power was thought to come from Deneb."

An angry peal from the linkbox. "That is self-evidently false," sang the cool voice of Sister Delta Four. "No star possesses any such power to share. No mind in the universe is more powerful than the Machine."

She paused while the black box snarled again. "If the falsehood is Harry Hickson's, the truth will be extracted when he is captured," she translated sweetly. "If the falsehood is yours, Major Gann, you are in grave danger of the Body Bank."

He cried, "I'm telling the truth! I'm loyal to the Plan of Man!"

The box sang; the girl intoned, "The Machine rejects such merely verbal assurances. One moment. The Machine is receiving additional data through another input."

Queerly, the girl's voice was fading. Gann blinked at her. She seemed to be moving—dwindling—as if she were falling away from him, down through the long, dark emptiness of space. It was as if Gann were looking at her through a zoom lens, pulling away. She receded a thousand yards . . .

Then she was back. Gann felt a moment's vertigo, as if the Planner's suite down in the bowels of the earth were somehow dancing a slow waltz. The feeling passed.

The linkbox whirred menacingly, and Sister Delta Four sang, "The Machine terminates this interview." A sharp hum from the linkbox. "It reminds you that unplanned ideas, like unplanned words and unplanned actions, must be severely corrected. But it reserves judgment on your ultimate disposition."

Her white, perfect face was smiling slightly, perhaps in contemplation of her instant rapture that was soon to come, when the buried electrodes would excite her brain to the incomparable bliss of electronic communion. But the linkbox was not yet through with her. It buzzed again, harshly.

"The Machine finds your narrative incomplete," she recited melodiously, contemplating Gann with her dark, serene eyes. "You have not identified the Starchild. You have revealed no facts about the *Togethership*. You have not accounted for the so-called Writ of Liberation. You have not explained how you got into the vault of the Machine."

Gann shook his head. "I don't know what to tell you," he said. The box whirred implacably.

"Your statements are inadequate," Sister Delta Four sang again. "But the interview is concluded . . ."

There was that surge of unreal motion again. Gann gripped his chair. This time even the girl felt it; her perfect lips opened, her eyes shook a flicker of surprise.

The linkbox twittered urgently. At the same moment

loud bells and sirens began to sound elsewhere in the Planner's warrens.

"Earth temblors," the girl began haltingly, "have been detected at several points . . ."

Then the linkbox crashed out a loud, despairing sound. Sister Delta Four gasped. Instinctively she reached out and caught Boysie Gann's arm. "Pyropods!" she cried. "The . . . the . . . Oh, you've got to help! The Planner's hall has been invaded by pyropods! Dozens of them! They're there now!"

The private room in which Sister Delta Four had been interrogating Boysie Gann was one tiny office in the immense network of corridors and chambers that was the administrative and living headquarters of the Planner. It had been locked, but the door opened instantly to the pattern of the girl's fingertips on the knob. It flung wide, and Gann and the girl ran through the open doorway, into a wide, gold-walled hall. Broad as a highway, tall as a two-story building, it ran straight through the heart of a mountain, the Planner's rooms opening off it at intervals all the way. It was a great ceremonial thoroughfare, lined with glittering gold and crystal statuary, hung in gold brocades, paneled with murals and viewscreens.

And it was filled with the reeking, choking, dusty smoke of jet exhausts.

A scream of some huge rocketing body ripping through the air smote their ears. A human shout of anguish—the cries of men taken by surprise—the thin, ear-splitting volley of laser guns. In all the noise and confusion Gann saw one thing clearly—saw it, grabbed the girl by her arm and pulled her back into the shelter of the doorway.

A pyropod was rocketing toward them down the hall.

It roared at them at a speed nearing Mach One; in the cramped quarters of the hall the shriek of its passage was physically painful, deafening. And the look of the thing was that of an avenging angel come to Earth, set on destruction.

It was a nightmare come to life. Wilder than the most fantastic of the Planner's toys, it was shaped a little like a scorpion, larger than a charging buffalo. Its eyes were great mirrors with stalked receptors at the center—natural radio telescopes, glowing red. Its jaws were mighty enough to crunch steel bars. Its talons could rip through armor plate. Its body was armored with darkly shining scales; a long, wicked, saber-like tail was arched over its back. And the whole thing was screaming through the air of the tunnel toward them.

The girl cried out in fear; Gann pulled her head against his chest, quieting her—though in truth the sound of her terror was lost in the ear-splitting din of the pyropod's passage. This was no baby, like the one Gann had played with on Harry Hickson's reef. It was an armored juggernaut, full-grown, capable of battling a Plan space cruiser on equal terms.

It passed them and rocketed into a group of armed guardsmen, knotted a hundred yards down the hall. They were firing wildly with laser and projectile weapons; it struck them, passed . . . and they were gone. Only a jackstraw heap of corpses and stirring near-dead marked where they had been.

"Great Machine!" gasped Sister Delta Four, her impeccable serenity gone, her black hood thrown back, the bright metal plaque blinking out of a terrified face. "What was that?"

"You told me," snapped Gann. "Pyropod! If it comes back, we're dead!"

She whimpered and tugged at his arm. "Back in here . . . we can hide."

"No! There are others. If one finds us this way we don't have a chance. But if I can get a gun . . ."

He stared down the broad, long hall. The bright jet

of the pyropod's tail was out of sight. Perhaps the monster had gone into another room, or down another hallway. Meanwhile, the guardsmen were still in a heap of death.

He came to a fast decision. "Julie—I mean . . . oh, never mind that. Listen! These things can be killed if you know where to aim. I'm going after a gun. You stay in the room!" And he was off, running as hard as he could, straight down the broad hall toward the dying men. He fought the temptation to skulk along the sides. There was no concealment here. If the creature came back, he would be dead; it was that simple. His only chance was speed. He did that hundred yards in Olympic time.

And it was nearly too slow, at that. Gasping, wheezing, his chest and muscles on fire, he heard a sudden growing volume of sound and looked up. A howl of sound was coming toward him, and behind it, almost as fast as the sound itself, a pyropod was rocketing at him.

He flung himself to the floor.

The thing missed him by inches; he caught a quick glimpse of metal jaws and crystal tusks, of enormous talons reaching out for him; then it was past, and he was up and running.

He heard the thing crashing, smashing, battering into the statuary and the walls of the hall, stopping itself at heedless cost, but he did not turn. He leaped to the fallen guardsmen, caught up a laser gun, checked its charge and whirled.

The pyropod had completed its turn.

It caught Gann in its pulsing red headlamps. It was screaming at him, a living battle rocket. He fired one maximum-blast shot into its eye, and tumbled to the ground again.

It screamed in agony as it passed over him. It blundered blindly into a wall, sideswiped a cluster of statuary, gouged out a bright streak in the hard metal of the corridor. Its jet flamed brightly and faded. Gann fired one more shot, then covered his head with his hands.

There was a great distant explosion. He felt the shock waves pass over him. Some of the corpses near him were stirred by the thrust of it, their bleeding limbs flopping wildly, their unseeing faces nodding.

The pyropod was gone.

But Sister Delta Four had said "dozens" of them . . .

Quickly Gann stooped to the abattoir the pyropod had left and rummaged for weapons. He discovered a half-empty laser weapon, pocketed a light projectile gun, loaded up with the three heaviest-charge laser guns he could find. Then he turned to go after Sister Delta Four.

She was standing just behind him. She had seen what he was doing, and she had done the same. She held two weapons, and in a pouch in her robes Gann could see the glitter of at least one more.

He hesitated, then grinned.

"Come on," he cried. "Let's see what we can do! Right in the eyes, remember!" He clapped her on the shoulder, and turned and ran in the direction of the Great Hall of the Planner.

A hellish howling and roaring led him to it. He needed no other signs.

Before he got there, he destroyed two more pyropods, neither quite as big as the one that had nearly got them in the hall, and Sister Delta Four had frightened another off with a long-range shot that might or might not have hit.

The Great Hall of the Planner was the mother hive. It was filled with the great creatures, ripping through the smoky, sulfurous air, ripping out boulder-sized bits from the walls, from the huge golden chair of the Planner, from anything that would give them reaction mass. They seemed to have conquered the human defenders of the

Hall with no trouble, and were fighting among themselves over the spoils.

Then Gann caught the slim ruby flash of a laser weapon.

One of the pyropods bellowed with pain, like an air-raid siren gone mad. It was not a mortal wound, but it must have been an agonizing one; the injured creature hurtled through the air and collided with another feasting beast; the two began to slash each other.

Someone was still alive in the room!

Warning the girl to remain behind, Gann peered cautiously around the door. The laser flash had seemed to come from one of the decorative niches holding statuary, under a painted lunette. Gann took a deep breath and shouted, then ducked back around the door. But it was useless. In the monstrous racket of the snarling, fighting pyropods his voice was unheard.

He caught Sister Delta Four by the shoulder, pulled her close to him so that her ear was next to his lips. "I'm going to try to pick them off one by one!" he cried. "They're not paying any attention right now. I think I can get most of them. But if any start this way, you shoot right for the eyes!"

She nodded, her face calm and untouched again, the great service lasers incongruous in her hands. He gave her a last thoughtful glance, unable to forget the bright communion plate that was now once again hidden under the black cowl, then turned toward the Great Hall.

It took him twenty minutes.

He counted, and there were fifteen of the great beasts rocketing and fighting about the hall. He got seven of them, one by one, before there was any trouble. Then at Sister Delta Four's warning touch, he had to turn and destroy a lone wanderer racing toward them down the hall.

He got three more, and then he noticed that at the

far side of the hall one screamed, burst and died that he had not fired on. Whoever was hiding in the niche across the hall had seen what he was doing, and had copied him.

There were two guns firing then—no, three; for Sister Delta Four stepped out beside him and helped gun down the last survivors, confused and blundering, as the walls shook with the creatures' screams and the air grew acrid and sickening with their fumes.

Then they were all gone.

Hesitantly Gann entered the hall, laser guns ready, eyes darting about as he picked his way across the destroyed battleground.

There were distant bellowings still. Obviously there were still a few strays elsewhere in the underground palace of the Planner; but most of them were dead in this room. He hurried toward his unknown ally.

Machine General Abel Wheeler stepped stiffly out of the niche and moved toward him. There was a hard grin of victory on his face. He holstered one gun and thrust out a hand with a motion like a piston to grasp Gann's extended clasp. "Well done, Major," he rasped.

"Thank you, sir. I had help. This is—"

The general's expression did not change. "I know Sister Delta Four," he boomed. "You may tell the Machine that I commend you, Sister. Please contact the Machine now and ascertain its condition. I fear this attack may have been intended to harm it!"

He grasped Gann's arm in a grip of steel and led him away. "Ugly creatures," he rasped, kicking at one enormous ripped cadaver. "Poetic justice, you might say. The Planner has always been fascinated by them. Interesting coincidence that they've appeared out of nowhere, here in his own home grounds." He glanced over his shoulder at Sister Delta Four, who was quickly chiming her tonal beads, setting up her linkbox. "See here, Gann. Look at this."

On the floor in front of the niche where General Wheeler had taken refuge there was a square of thick, creamy paper. "What is it. sir?"

"Pick it up, man! See for yourself!"

There were human voices, now, coming from the hall. The mighty forces of the Plan of Man were regathering themselves. Order was being restored.

Boysie Gann hesitated. Something was wrong. "The Planner?" he asked. "Is he . . ." He looked around the great hall littered with the corpses of the invading pyropods and the human guards who had been trapped there.

"Not he, Major! Gone this half hour. Read that document!"

Gann, with a feeling that something was awry, leaned forward and retrieved the paper. He glanced at it.

Then the doubts and uncertainties dropped out of his mind. This paper was strangely familiar. He had seen one just like it—twenty billion miles away—in the hands of the dying Machine Colonel Zafar.

That had been the document they called the Writ of Liberation!

And this one was something almost as earthshaking in its importance, almost as dangerous to the Plan of Man.

Boysie Gann read swiftly, looked up at the silent carved face of General Wheeler wonderingly, then returned to the paper. It was headed *To the Planner,* and it said:

To the Planner, or to whoever succeeds him if he is now dead:

You and those who serve with you ignored my warning and discounted the dimming of the Sun.

I send you now a pack of beasts to show that my

powers can do more than frighten. They will destroy much. They may yet destroy more.

If I send them again, it will not be to the head-quarters of the Planner—if anything remains of that to be destroyed.

The next demonstration will occur in the vaults of the Planning Machine.

Gann looked up, his lips taut, his eyes narrowed. "The Planning Machine!" he said. "General, we must tell Sister Delta Four at once! This must be conveyed to the Machine immediately."

The general rasped, "That decision will be made by me, Major. What have you to say for yourself?"

Startled, Gann said, "Why—I don't know what you mean, General. I didn't have anything to do with . . ." Then he saw that the general was no longer standing with his arms at his side. One hand held a laser gun again, and it was pointing at him.

"You're under arrest," clipped General Wheeler metal-lically. "Do not attempt to draw those weapons. Do not speak or move."

Gann opened his mouth, then closed it again. This was the overwhelming, culminating insanity of a fantastic experience. Himself under arrest!

But for what? He dared not even ask. The general's iron expression showed that he meant his orders to be obeyed.

Behind him, Boysie Gann heard the movements of the guards, coming near—and past them, a distant booming.

He recognized that sound. Another stray pyropod! He forgot his orders and cried: "General! There's another one."

General Wheeler rapped, "Be silent! I will not speak again! The men will take care of your beast!" His voice was queerly loud, Gann thought, even in his confusion—

almost as if the general were speaking not to him, but to the roomful of witnesses.

But he could not help himself. He knew what one single pyropod could do, knew that even the Planner's guards might not be able to cope with it—and knew that in that room was the body and heart of the girl he loved, even though they might be inhabited by the cold, machinelike mind of Sister Delta Four. He whirled, drew his laser gun and was ready as the roar of the pyropod shrieked to the door of the room and the creature appeared.

Gann fired at the red eyes.

The guards were ready too, alerted by the sound and by Gann's quick action; they had turned and were firing. The creature was caught in a dozen bolts of destroying energy. It puffed into flame and exploded . . .

And between Gann and the door, Sister Delta Four, whispering into her linkbox, fell silently forward. She dropped to the floor and did not move, though the linkbox hooted questioningly to her.

"She's hit!" cried Gann and, dropping his weapons, raced to her. He caught her up in his arms, and stared into her black eyes.

His hands were covered with blood. Along one side of her black robes a spreading patch of sticky moisture began to seep, clouding the bright electronic symbols, trickling to the floor.

There was no heartbeat.

He raised his eyes, stared vacantly at the approaching General Wheeler. "Is she dead?" he demanded, unable to take it in. "Was it my shot? Or . . ." He paused, trying to remember. Had there been another pencil-thin lance of laser light coming from his side of the room? Had General Wheeler fired over his shoulder and shot Sister Delta Four?

But there was no time to think of that. The general was on him now, his face a metallic mask of sternness.

"Disarm that man!" he rasped to the guards. "Take him before the Planner! I accuse him of bringing this document here! I accuse him of admitting the beasts we have destroyed. I accuse him of slaying Sister Delta Four to keep her from denouncing him. I accuse him of being the Starchild!"

X

The battered veterans of the skirmish with the pyropods, limping out of the battlefield and taking the swift elevators to the surface, found the Planner standing like a jovial Santa Claus on a quartz-walled balcony, near the snowy summit of the mountain in which his headquarters was buried.

This was his eyrie, the great crow's-nest of his palace. He chuckled to General Wheeler, "They tried to get me and missed! They'll not have another chance! We'll wipe out every last lone rebel."

The general rasped, "Sir, here is your first traitor! This is the man who is responsible. I found him bearing this document."

Gann cried, "Planner, the general is lying! He knows I didn't—"

"Silence!" snapped the general.

The Planner did not even look at Gann. Smiling and nodding, he read the square of paper, then dropped it negligently to the floor. "You're sure he's the Starchild, General?" he asked.

"Consider the evidence, sir!" rapped the general. "One. He appeared originally in the vaults of the Machine, with no explanation of how he got there. Two. At the same time, the Writ of Liberation appeared, also unexplained.

Three. He was bearing this document when I apprehended him. Four. He displayed a suspicious knowledge of the vulnerable spots on the pyropods when his own life was in danger. Five. He purposely slew Sister Delta Four, making it look like an accident, so that she could not speak against him. Six. He was about to do the same to me when I ordered the guards to disarm him. The conclusion, sir, is overwhelmingly indicated that Machine Major Boysie Gann is indeed the Starchild."

"But, sir," cried Gann.

The Planner gestured, and one of the guards wrenched his arm, forcing him to be quiet. "That's better," chuckled the old Planner, beaming down on Boysie Gann. His dose of communion had clearly lasted him a long time; he was as bubbling with good humor as if the Machine even now were shooting pleasure sensations into his brain. "Yet," said the Planner, smiling good-humoredly at General Wheeler, "one of the guards reported that it was you, not Gann, who killed the sister. Could you have been mistaken?"

"No, sir! Impossible, sir. I had no reason."

The Planner nodded cheerfully and scratched his plump old cheek. He got to his feet and went to the quartz wall of his eyrie, squinting out into the sunset sky. To windward of the summit, the descending sun picked out a towering crown of cumulus. Beyond the crystal parapet, its last rays shimmered on a small waterfall and tinted the falling slopes of evergreens.

"As a matter of fact," the Planner added over his shoulder, "Sister Delta Four is not dead." He stared smiling down the slopes toward a brown-smogged city below. "She is now in surgery. Her heart was destroyed, but circulation was restored before the brain was damaged. Even now a donor is being provided to replace her lost parts."

Boysie Gann cried joyfully, "Plan be thanked! Sir, she'll

tell you that I knew nothing of the pyropods until she herself told me about them!"

"Silence!" rasped General Wheeler. "Guards! Your orders are to keep him quiet. I understand donors are needed for several of your wounded comrades. The first man who fails to keep the prisoner silent will be considered a volunteer!"

"Not so fast," said the Planner, chuckling. "Your zeal goes too far, General." His heavy-lidded eyes looked dark and as old as the lichen-crusted stone below the crystal wall as he gazed benignly toward the far city in the smog. "Let us Plan," he said, turning and smiling. "Let us decide what to do."

The Vice-Planner for Venus spoke up promptly: "Double the guards in the vaults of the Machine, sir. Institute maximum security measures, admitting no unauthorized person . . ." He broke off and scratched his enormous nose in puzzlement as he realized that neither Boysie Gann nor the pyropods had submitted to security check before entering the most heavily guarded places in the Plan of Man.

A male acolyte in the black robes of the Machine, listening to a subdued buzzing from his linkbox, raised his voice suddenly. "The Machine requires the services of the prisoner," he chanted. "The Machine instructs Machine General Wheeler that the prisoner is not to be harmed in any way that will affect his memory or his intellect."

Wheeler's expression was that of a steel-gray thundercloud. The Planner turned toward him, chuckling. "You have your orders, General," he said good-humoredly. "Be sure they are carried out. Do you know what those orders are, young man?" he added, turning with a bland expression of cheer to Boysie Gann.

"No, sir. But I stand ready to serve the Plan of Man!"

"Oh, you do indeed," nodded the Planner. "In a very

special way, as it happens. Major, you have been selected to replace Sister Delta Four. The Machine is about to permit you to receive training in its special service as an acolyte—and then communion!"

The heavy iron security collar was not enough for so precious an enemy of the Plan as Boysie Gann.

"You're not just a Risk," one of the guards explained solicitously. "See, we can't take a chance, Major. We don't want to blow your little head off. We don't want to kill you. We want to deliver you in one piece, right? So just stand still there while we put these cuffs on you . . . and we'll take you to the training base . . . and then, when the Machine's all finished with you, *then* we'll blow your head off!" And the guard snapped the fetters cruelly tight on Gann's wrists and started him moving with a shove.

They took him to a subtrain station first, and would not answer his questions. Was Julie Martinet all right? Why had General Wheeler lied? What was the Machine going to do with him? To each question there was only one response: "Shut up, you! Move on!"

But then there was nowhere to move. They were in the subtrain station, the great cold, vaulted shed where the enormous electron-flow-driven globes waited to carry their passengers through tunnels in the earth, across a continent or under a sea. But no globe was moving.

They brought Gann to a platform, ten security guards forming the detail that surrounded him; then they waited. Boysie Gann could see that the station was a military base, because of the armored guard boxes beside the troughs, and because of the black Technicorps uniforms on everyone. That was understandable enough; this was the depot that served the Planner himself, the one nearest his tunneled-out mountain retreat. But what was not understandable was that there were neither arrivals nor departures.

Behind him, a track lock closed with a wheeze of leaking air. A Togetherness girl froze her automatic smile as she caught sight of his collar, and hurried past. The guards in their radar horns gazed vacantly after her.

"Look," said Boysie Gann, "what's the matter? What are we waiting for?"

"Shut up, you," growled a Machine Sergeant of the guards. But he had a worried look. One of his men said something to him; the sergeant replied in an undertone. All Gann could catch was: ". . . trouble in the tunnels somewhere. Now shut up. When they're ready for us, we'll know."

The great forty-foot bubbles waited silently in their passage cradles, and Boysie Gann stood regarding them. Wherever he was going, it was probably somewhere far away. Short-haul trips were seldom by way of the subtrains. The great atomic drills of the Plan had tunneled straight-line passages from all major centers to all others, sometimes relayed, sometimes piercing nearly through the nickel-iron core of the Earth itself in a single non-stop thrust from Sidney, say, to Calcutta. The great freight and passenger globes reached speeds so great that Coriolis force was their principal adversary; the electrostatic hoops that banded the evacuated tunnels were double and triple strength on the side against which the earth's rotation tended to throw the spheres. Via the subtrains, no point on Earth was more than a few hours away from any other . . .

Boysie Gann became aware of a confused mutter of excitement, and focused his eyes on what was going on in the subtrain shed. A great dull freightsphere was sliding gently into the station, emerging from the mouth of a belt-ringed tunnel.

"About time they got 'em going again," grumbled the

Machine Sergeant. "All right, let's move out. They'll be letting us board now."

The sergeant was right. Within ten minutes they were in a subtrain globe, settling down in a passenger compartment. But there was a wait of nearly a quarter of an hour more before Boysie Gann felt the gentle lurch that meant they had begun to move.

His guards were more relaxed, now that they were in the subtrain. Gann could not very well escape them now, not when there was nowhere to go but the interior of a forty-foot sphere, with nothing outside but great electrostatic hoops in an airless tunnel, whizzing by at speeds of thousands of miles an hour. A couple of the guards disappeared, came back with self-satisfied smiles, and relieved the others. Clearly there was a Togetherness canteen on the globe. Even the radar-horned sergeant looked somehow less inimical, more like a human being.

Above all things, Gann wished he knew what had happened to Sister Delta Four. There had been a moment there, while the pyropods were attacking, when she had seemed less like a cold-hearted servant of the Machine and more like the girl he had kissed at Playa Blanca. He dreamed of getting her back—of somehow winning favor with the Machine and receiving the great reward of Julie Martinet's release . . .

It was only a dream. Considering his position now, it was an insane one.

Gann realized that he should be devoting every second's thought he could to planning—to trying to understand what had put him in this position, and what he could do. But it seemed quite hopeless. He had the giddy sensation that the universe had gone mad. From that first moment on Polaris Station, when he had followed Machine Colonel Zafar down to the methane snowball, events had carried him helplessly along; they made no sense to him, but there was nothing he could do to help interpret them. Their incomprehensibility was intrinsic. It was not that he was lacking in comprehension, it was that the things which had happened were not to be understood in the sane, sensible terms of life under the Plan of Man. . . .

He felt a giddy sensation again, and this time it was not in his mind.

Boysie Gann leaped to his feet in alarm. He could not help thinking of the strange queasiness that had preceded his twenty-billion-mile drop into the Planning Machine's catacombs . . . the same sensation, just before the pyropods struck . . .

But this was not the same thing at all. The lurching, twisting sensation he felt was simply explained. The subtrain car had come to a stop. It was hanging now, spinning slowly, between the charged hoops of its airless tunnel.

If Gann had been in any doubt, the cries from outside his room, the shouts of guards within, removed that doubt quickly. Everyone on the subtrain globe seemed to be shouting at once. "What's the matter?" "We've stopped!" "Great Plan, we're a couple of hundred miles down! The temperature—" "Help me! Let me out of here!" The voices were a confused babble, but they all had in common the warning knife edge of panic. There was terror on that subtrain car—terror that could not be calmed with words, for its base was all too real.

The Machine Sergeant comprehended the situation at once. With a jerk of his radar-horned head he bawled at his squad: "Come on, outside! Those sheep'll stampede if we don't keep 'em in line!"

Boysie Gann was left alone. Outside he could hear the Technicorps guards shouting orders at the terrified travelers on the subtrain. No one seemed to know what had happened. They had stopped; that was all. Hundreds of miles below the surface of the earth, the rock outside hot enough to melt aluminum, the pressure great enough to crush diamonds into dust if the electrostatic hoops ever faltered—they were stopped. Whatever it was that had disrupted the service before they left the station was probably disrupting it again.

The only difference was that now they were where no help could ever reach them, where if the fields in the hoops failed they would be dead in the least fraction of a second—where even if the field maintained itself they would be dead in a few days of asphyxiation, unless they could move.

Then, abruptly, there was another lurch, and they were moving again.

As the great forty-foot sphere gathered speed and stability, Boysie Gann became aware that he had been hardly breathing. There was a great cry of thanksgiving from the people outside his room. One by one his guards came back, chattering and laughing, seeming almost human. They did not include him in their conversation, but they did not go out of their way to keep him out. One of them even disappeared for a few minutes, then came back with a tray of drinks from the Togetherness canteen . . .

And then the great globe shook again. Shook—crashed into something that shrieked of destroyed metal— slammed to a jolting, smashing stop. Gann and the guards tumbled across the room, hurled against the wall like thrown gravel.

Boysie Gann heard screams and a rending sound of the metal of the great sphere being crushed. "We've had it!" someone shrieked. "The fields have failed!" And as he went deep into black oblivion (not yet feeling pain but knowing that he was bleeding; he had struck the wall too hard to get up and walk away), Gann had time for one last thought: *He's right,* thought Gann; *this is the end.*

When, some indeterminate time later, he opened his eyes and found himself still alive, he was almost disappointed. Gann was in an emergency hospital. Stiff white bandages covered part of his eyes; his head ached as if a corps of drummers were using it for practice; he could see, under the shadow of the bandages, that one arm was encased in a balloon-cast.

But he was alive.

A Togetherness nurse was bending over him. He said clearly, "I thought the tube collapsed."

"Hush," she said gently. "It did. But you were almost at the surface, and the wrecking squads dug you out."

"Almost at the surface?" He squinted past her at the second figure standing by his bed. For one crazy instant on waking he had thought it was the Angel of Death come to take him away. Now he saw it was an acolyte of the Machine, the linkbox in her hand, whispering tinkling notes to the microphone it contained. "I—I guess I'm at the training center," he said.

The nurse nodded. "Sleep if you can," she ordered. And Boysie Gann was glad to comply . . .

For three days Boysie Gann had the status of a convalescent. It was a considerable improvement over his status as a major public enemy.

The immediate guard detail was withdrawn—several had been killed in the tube implosion and were going through the messy business of resuscitation and repair at the Body Bank. Gann was free to wander within the limited confines of one wing of the hospital in which he was a patient.

He was even allowed access to the recreation lounge, run by a young Togetherness girl who reminded him of Quarla Snow. Her disposition was like Quarla's, too. She did not seem conscious of his collar. Most important, she let him watch the news-screens to his heart's content.

Boysie Gann had been away from Earth, off on the Reefs or in intensive custody, for so long that he had lost touch with the running news stories.

He sat and dreamed. What was happening on the screen soaked slowly into his mind and heart. He watched, and loved, the gold-haired, long-legged choruses of Togetherness girls cooing their gentle threats: "Work for the Plan! Live for the Plan! *You* don't want to go to Heaven and make spare parts for the Plan!" Though he knew his chances of winding up in the Body Bank called Heaven and making "spare parts for the Plan" must be rated pretty high, there was no fear in what the girls were singing. It was a part of a life that he had lost, and he wanted it back.

Above all, he wanted to find himself again.

Boysie Gann could not recognize himself in the enemy of the Machine who had been castigated by the Planner himself, denounced by Machine General Wheeler, interrogated by Sister Delta Four. That Boysie Gann was a creature who had been born on Polaris Station, a man who lived with undead Reef rats and queer creatures called spacelings and pyropods. Gann could not fit the strange, rebellious shape of this other Boysie Gann into his personality, could not add the two identities and produce a vector sum of his future life . . .

He sat up straight and glared at the viewscreen.

He had been watching a worldwide news broadcast with half his mind, hardly conscious of what he saw, although in fact what he saw was exciting enough. The news broadcast was almost a catalogue of disasters—a crashed Plan cruiser that destroyed half a city, earthquakes in Antarctica, a runaway nuclear reactor on the Indian subcontinent. Then there had been a nearer disaster. The screen had shown the very subtrain catastrophe that had put him in this place.

And called it sabotage!

Gann blinked. He hardly recognized the accident. The bland, fat Technicolonel puffing out his gruff charges of criminal conspiracy seemed to be talking about some other disaster, on some other world. Malicious sabotage? A bomb planted in the subtrain to discredit the Planner and the Planning Machine? Most incongruous of all, *himself* as the archvillain, with the radar-horned guard sergeant as his accomplice?

Gann put down his glass of vitamin-laced fruit juice and hobbled over to the Togetherness girl in charge of the lounge.

He was shaking. "Please," he begged. "Did you see that? What is it all about?"

She scolded him sunnily. "Now, now! Your duty under the Plan is to get well! You must prepare yourself to return to serve. No questions, no worries—nothing but healing and rest!"

He said with difficulty, "It said on the newscast that I was responsible for the subtrain accident. It isn't so! And the guard sergeant who was in charge of me—what happened to him?"

Her large, clear eyes darkened for a moment in puzzlement. But only for a moment. She would not question her orders; if her orders said that she was to care for an enemy of the Plan, she would care for an enemy of the Plan. She shook her head and, smiling, led him back to the couch. "Drink your juice," she said with playful severity, and would say no more. To her, what the Plan of Man ordained was necessarily right and true—because "right" and "truth" were defined by the Plan of Man.

Or so thought Boysie Gann.

So thought Boysie Gann, and was aware in some part of him that there was something in that thought which was dangerous—dangerous to him and to all mankind

—for if the sweet and empty-headed Togetherness girl accepted the Plan so unquestioningly . . .

He could not put the thought together. It almost seemed as if he himself, and General Wheeler, and even the Planner—as if all the human race within the Plan were in some sense no less empty-headed than a Togetherness girl.

But he could not complete the thought. And then time ran out and he no longer had leisure for such thoughts, for he began the course of training that would lead him to communion with the Machine.

Dyadic relation: *I hate spinach.* Ternary relation: *I hate spinach except when it is well washed.* Quaternary relation: *I hate spinach except when it is well washed because the sand gets in my teeth.*

With instructor and book, with constant subliminal tapes droning while he slept and teaching machines snapping at him awake, Boysie Gann began to learn the calculus of statement, the logic of relations, the geometries of Hilbert and Ackermann and Boole. Conjunctions and disjunctions, axioms and theorems, double negations and metastatements . . . they all surged through his brain, nesting with destructive dilemmas and syllogisms in the mood of Barbara. He learned to transpose and commute. He learned the principle of exportation and the use of dots as brackets. He learned the unambiguous phrasing and inflectionless grammar of machine programming; he learned the distinction between perceptual symbols and motor symbols, and learned to make the auditory symbols that bridged the gap. For hours with an oscillator squeal beeping in his ear to guide him, he sang endless quarter-tone scales. He studied the factorization problems of the General Problem Solver and learned to quantify relationships. He learned the construction of truth tables, and how to use them to track down tautologies in a premise.

There were neither classes nor schoolrooms; there were only study and work. It went on and on, endlessly. Gann woke to the drone of the tape-recorded voice under his pillow, ate with the chime of sonic bells in his ear, fell exhausted into his bed with schematics of shared-time computer inputs racing through his mind.

There was a world outside the training center, but he had lost touch with it completely. In stolen moments he caught snatches of conversation between his few human contacts—the Togetherness girls who served him at table, the guards who roamed the halls—that his mind was too hard-pressed to fit together. The Starchild. The Writ of Liberation. Disasters under the earth; rocket explosions in space. They did not matter; what mattered was null hypotheses and probabilistic calculus. If he had time enough, and thought enough, to probe beyond the demands of the training, his mind always reached one step ahead—to the moment when training was over and he would receive the metal badge of communion in his flesh—and it recoiled, and returned to Hilbert and Boole.

When the course was over, Gann did not realize it. He went to sleep—exhausted, as he was always exhausted in this place. He tumbled into the narrow, hard bed in the solitary, tile-walled room. The voice under his pillow promptly began to recite to him:

". . . generate a matrix K, utilizing the mechanism of associative retrieval to add contextual relationships to coordinate retrieval. Let the ith row and the jth column show the degree of association . . ."

Some part of him was taking it in, he knew, but his conscious mind was hardly aware of it. All he was aware of was his own inadequacy. He would never match the pure, crystalline tones of Sister Delta Four and the other acolytes. He did not have the voice for it. He would never grasp and retain all the information theory and programming he had been taught. He did not have the training for it. . . .

He drifted off to sleep.

His cot was hard. The barracks were like an air-conditioned vault. Every night at lights-out it held eighty tired and silent trainees, every cot filled. And each morning, the harsh clanging of the reveille gong found a few cots empty.

No one spoke of the missing trainees. Their gear was gone with them, from the narrow shelves above the cots. Their names had been erased from the company rolls. They had ceased to exist. Nobody asked why.

One night, however, the shuffle of hurried feet awakened him. With a gasp of wild alarm, he sat up on his cot.

"Jim?" He whispered the name of the man in the next bunk, a new recruit, who had the physique of a wrestler and a pure tenor voice. His mother had been a Togetherness singer, and his father had died for the Plan in space. "What—?"

"You're asleep, bud," a harsh whisper rasped in the dark. "Better stay that way."

A heavy hand caught his shoulder, shoved him down.

Gann wanted to help, but he was afraid. He watched as dark forms closed around the cot. He heard Jim's stifled gasp. He heard a muffled rattle of a voice. He heard the rustle of clothing, a metallic clink. The cot creaked. He closed his eyes as a thin blade of light stabbed at his face. Footsteps padded away.

He lay a long time in the dark, listening to the breath sounds of fewer than eighty sleeping men. Jim had treasured that red plastic medal that said his father had been a Hero of the Plan, Second Class. Jim's voice had been fine and true, but he had been too slow to learn the semantic calculus.

Gann wanted to help, but there was nothing he could

do. The Machine required something mechanical in its selected servants; perhaps Jim had not been quite mechanical enough. Gann turned on the hard cot and began repeating to himself the semantic tensors; presently he slept again.

XI

Two days later, entering the second phase of training, Gann remembered the first phase through a fog of exhaustion as something like a week end at a Togetherness beach hostel. The pressure never stopped.

"Look Mechanical!"

Bleak-voiced instructors hammered that injunction at him. Bright-eyed Togetherness girls cooed it to him, as he shuffled through the chow lines. Blazing stereo signs burned it into his retinas. Sleepless speakers whispered it endlessly under his pillow.

"Look Mechanical! . . . Act Mechanical! . . . Be Mechanical!"

Each rasping sergeant and murmuring girl pointed out what that meant. To master the myriad difficult tone phonemes of Mechanese, a man had to become mechanical. The searing signs and the whispering speakers reminded him that those who failed went promptly to the Body Bank.

Locked in a stifling little examination cell walled with gray acoustic padding, he sat hunched over a black linkbox, straining to catch the fleeting inflections of its tinkling Mechanese.

"The candidate—" Even that word almost escaped him. "The candidate will identify himself."

His answering voice came out too harsh and too high. He gulped to clear his throat, and stroked his tonal beads.

"Candidate Boysie Gann." He swallowed again, and sang his serial number.

"Candidate Boysie Gann, you are under examination," the box purred instantly. "A passing score will move you one stage farther toward that high service which the Plan rewards with communion. But you must be warned that you are now beyond the point of return! The Plan has no place for rejects, with your classified knowledge and training—except in the salvage centers."

"I understand, and I live to serve." He sang the single difficult phoneme.

"Then the test will begin," the box chirped. "You will answer each question clearly and fully, in correct Mechanese. Each millisecond of delay and each tone defect will be scored against you. The Plan has no time to waste, nor space for error. Are you ready to begin?"

Hurriedly, he sang the tone that said, "I am ready to begin."

"Your response was delayed nine milliseconds beyond the optimum point," the box whined instantly. "Your initial tone was twelve cycles too high. Your tonal glide was abrupt and irregular. The duration of your utterance was one millisecond too long. These errors will be scored against you."

"I understand."

"That response was not required from you," the box snarled. "Your errors, however, have been analyzed and graphed. You will now prepare for your initial test question. . . . What is the first principle of mechanized learning?"

When he first tried to sing his answer, his voice came out too hoarse and too low. The box piped out a new total cumulative error before he had time to touch the beads to find the true tone and try again.

"Learning is action," his uneven tones came out at last. "That is the first principle of mechanized instruction. Right responses must be instantly reinforced. Wrong responses must be instantly inhibited. The first equation of mechanized instruction states that efficiency of learning varies inversely with the time elapsed between response and reward."

"Your accumulated total error is now four hundred and eighty-nine points," the box snarled. "You will prepare for the next question. . . . What is the second principle of mechanized instruction?"

He was sweating now as he crouched on the hard little seat. The small gray room seemed too small. The padded walls pressed in upon him. He felt almost suffocated, and he had to gasp for the breath for his hurried reply.

"Learning is survival," he sang the curt phonemes, trying to cut them off correctly. "Successful learning is the adaptive way to life. Failure to learn is individual death. The second equation of mechanized instruction states that the speed of learning varies directly with the magnitudes of reward and punishment."

When he paused, the box chirped. Even to his straining ears, it was only a sharp metallic insect note, entirely meaningless. He had to whistle a request for the Machine to repeat.

"Your failure in reception scores ninety points against you." The notes from the box were only slightly slower and more intelligible. "Your cumulative total is now six hundred and seventy-three points. Your right-wrong ratio has fallen into the danger zone."

The racing tinkle of merciless notes, sharp as shattering glass, gave him no time to recover his shattered confidence. He was only dimly conscious of the itching tickle of sweat on his ribs, the cold tingle of sweat on his forehead, the sting of sweat in his eyes.

"You will prepare for your next question." That was

only a single gliding tone phoneme, gone in a few milliseconds, so brief he nearly missed it. "What is the third principle of mechanized instruction?"

He touched his beads for the tonal keys, and sang the required phonemes. "The third principle of mechanized instruction states that the greatest reward is the end of pain." His accumulated error mounted, and the merciless box demanded another principle of mechanized instruction—and yet another.

"Your test is ended," the box announced at last. "Your total accumulated error is five thousand nine hundred and forty points. You will report that total to your training group."

He was late when he reached his barracks to punch that total into the group computer. He was late again, half a minute late, for the calisthenics formation—a crime against the Machine which earned him two extra laps of double time in the track tunnel. The last man in the chow line, he was too tired to eat his ration when at last he reached the table with it; the wasted food cost him two yellow demerit points. When he got to his bunk at last, he felt too tired to sleep.

"Candidate Gann!"

He had not seen the dark forms approach his cot. He gasped and sat up trembling. A pale needle of light picked out his uniform, his boots, and kit and gear. A harsh whisper directed him. In a moment he was shuffling down the shadowy aisle between the heavy-breathing trainees, his kit on his back.

So this was it? For a moment his knees wobbled; then he began to feel illogically relieved.

He was almost yearning for the anesthesia of the Body Bank; he was almost hungry for oblivion. Because there wouldn't be any linkboxes in the Body Bank. He wouldn't have to practice any more impossible scales, or learn any more tables of semantic variation.

He was out of it all.

His black-uniformed escorts let him sit with them at a table in a nearly deserted mess hall. A sleepy Togetherness girl yawned as she served them. He ate no food. He drank two cups of black coffee that left a lingering bitterness in his mouth.

He joined five other stunned and sleepy trainees who must have come from another barracks. They carried their gear into a military subtrain, and carried it off again. They marched past a scowling sentry into another cavernous training center.

Gann left his gear in a tiny tile-walled cell and reported to a cadaverous Machine Major who wore the piebald scars of a Venusian anaerobic parasite. The major returned his salute stiffly, with a black-gloved hand.

"Congratulations, Major Gann."

Staring at the gaunt major who was shuffling through papers on his desk, Gann saw that the neat black glove was no glove, but the black skin of a salvaged hand.

"You have successfully completed Phase Two of your service training in Mechanese." Peering at that black, borrowed hand, Gann scarcely heard the words. "You have been assigned here for Phase Three, which consists of mechanized instruction."

A faint smile twisted the major's yellow patched face.

"Your test scores were unusual, Major Gann," he added. "The Machine has commended you. You ought to be a proud and happy man."

Gann had swayed backward when that cold fact struck him. He was not a proud and happy man. He stood speechless, breathless, shuddering with a secret horror.

"You have come a long way, Major Gann." The yellow scars turned the major's smile into a rictus of agony. "You have escaped the danger of salvage. You have moved far toward the highest reward." Wistfully his black fingers touched his own seamed and mottled forehead, where he had no communion receptacle of his own. "You are very fortunate, Major Gann!"

Gann stood swaying. Suddenly the harsh-lit room and the gray-cased computers and the piebald major seemed unreal. Terribly real, in his own spinning mind, the cold, bright scalpels and saws of the surgeons were carving out space for the socket in his own forehead. They were drilling into the crown and the temples and the base of his shaven head. They were probing with thin, cruel needles for the centers of sensation. They were coldly violating the most secret privacy of all his being. . . .

He wanted to scream.

"Is something wrong, Major Gann?" The gaunt major rose anxiously. "You look ill."

"Nothing, sir." Groping for himself, he grinned faintly. "You see, I didn't know that I had passed Phase Two. I thought we were in a salvage center."

"You'll soon get over that." The major's rictus grew more hideous. "With your record, you're as good as already wired for communion. I wish I were in your place."

"Thank—" He tried to wet the sandpaper dryness in his mouth and throat. "Thank you, sir!"

The Mechanese trainer was a ten-foot pear shape, fabricated out of bright aluminum. Swung in massive gimbals of gray-painted steel, it stood in a windy, gloomy cavern, under a water-stained concrete vault. Thick black cables and hoses snaked from it to the gray-cased control console at the tunnel mouth.

"There she is, sir!" The instructor was a plump young Techtenant with a pink baby face, wide blue eyes, and a bright communion plate set in his forehead. "The perfect teaching machine!"

Gann was queerly unsure of that. Smeared all over with a sticky jelly, wearing only loose gray coveralls, he hesitated at the tunnel mouth, staring uncomfortably up at that huge metal pear.

"Step right up, sir." The Techtenant gave him an innocent grin. "Strip off your robe and slip right in." The round blue eyes flickered at him inquiringly. "All ready, sir?"

He was wet and clammy with the jelly, and the coveralls were thin. Suddenly he shivered in the cold steady wind that blew out of the tunnel. He didn't really want to learn Mechanese. He didn't want to be rewarded with electrodes in his brain. But he gulped and said that he was ready.

The Techtenant touched something on the console. Air valves wheezed. That great metal pear tipped in the gimbals, opening like a sliced fruit. He stared at it, frozen, tingling, fascinated.

"Move ahead, sir." The Techtenant touched his shoulder respectfully. "Up the ladder. Strip off. Just lie down on the sensor-effector sheath." He chuckled easily. "Most students are a bit uneasy at first, but you'll find it fits you, sir."

Gann caught his breath and climbed the metal ladder. The rungs felt cold and sticky to his naked feet. The wind blew cold on his shaven head, and a sudden bitter taste of stale coffee came back from his stomach into his throat.

He stripped off the coveralls and crept uneasily out upon the bright pink membrane that lined the pear. It rippled beneath him, warm and slimy and almost alive, propelling his naked body into its central cavity.

"All set, sir?"

He attempted no answer to that cheery hail, but he heard another hiss of escaping air. The hinged upper half of the pear closed down. Warm constrictions of that pliant membrane caressed him into place. Total darkness seized him, in a hot and suffocating grip.

He tried to scream, and had no breath . . .

But then there was air for his lungs. He saw a pink glow of light through his closed eyelids.

He opened them, and saw Sister Delta Four.

Really, he supposed, it must have been only a projected image of her, but she looked alive enough. He knew this had to be an image because she wasn't in the buried training center. But she seemed to be. Robed and hooded and carrying her black link box, she was walking down a palm-fringed coral beach that looked queerly like the Togetherness center at Playa Blanca.

And he was walking with her.

The clinging effectors of the trainer duplicated every sensation: the hard, cold, yielding firmness of the wet sand, the tingling heat of the high sun, a cool puff of ocean breeze. He heard the dull boom of surf against the breakwater, and caught a sharp whiff of rotting seaweed and then a hint of Julie's perfume—for she was speaking to him now, in the warm, remembered tones of Julie Martinet.

"Here we are," she was saying, "for your first lesson in the Mechanese Learning Device, Mark Eight. This instrument is very nearly the last possible word in educational efficiency. If you co-operate, I'm sure you'll find the experience exciting and profitable." Her bright face smiled at him, tempting under the hood.

"Now," she said, "we are ready to begin your introduction to the technical vocabulary of Mechanese. It is built upon a principle of economy already familiar to you: one syllable for one sentence. Obviously, that requires a large number of syllables. The total vocabulary of Mechanese, as we compute it, is more than a billion monosyllables—more than a billion one-sound sentences."

He stopped on the beach—or it seemed that he did, for the synthetic experience created by the trainer had made him forget that he was anywhere else. Cold brine hissed over his bare feet, crumbled the hard sand beneath them, rushed back down the slope.

"I can't do it," he protested. "I can't memorize a billion words!"

Her soft laugh checked him. "You'll be surprised!" Her voice was a song, even when she spoke the old, familiar language. "You'll be surprised what the trainer can make you do." The sea breeze caught and lifted her hood, so that he had a sudden glimpse of the bright plate set in her forehead. Even in that mild tropic air, it made him cold and ill.

"Actually, though, you don't have to memorize a billion words," she said. "No more than a child has to memorize every possible sentence in English. All you must learn is how to construct the Mechanese monosyllables from combinations of a few thousand phonemes. You must learn to hear and understand very small distinctive variations in length and stress and pitch and a few other simple features of articulation."

"But I can't!" Feet planted in the wet sand, he waited until she turned back. He didn't want to learn, though he could scarcely tell her that. He was seeking secretly to defend himself from those cold probes that would be piercing his brain when he knew Mechanese. "I can't learn to utter a billion different words."

"You'll be surprised." Her laugh was as melodious as her voice. "Let's begin."

He shook his head stubbornly, trying to remind himself that the sharp white sand wasn't real, that the salt-scented wind wasn't real, that Julie herself wasn't real.

"Do co-operate," she urged him softly. "If you're a good student, we can go for a swim a little later on." Her eyes held a teasing promise, and her deft white hands made a fetching gesture, as if to toss away the robe and hood. "You must co-operate."

Her oval face turned suddenly sober.

"If you don't, you'll be sorry." Her voice turned slow and faint and sad. "I don't like to remind you of the third principle of mechanized instruction—but the greatest reward is the end of pain."

She shrugged, and her quick smile dazzled him. "Let's begin!"

They began with the verbal glides, the slight inflections of tone that meant tense and mood and voice and person and aspect. She trilled the difficult syllables. Trying faithfully to imitate them, he was soon reminded of the third law of mechanized learning.

Even the tiniest error brought a twinge of pain, and his errors were frequent and great. Even when he responded instantly with a phoneme that seemed to him precisely like the one she had uttered, it was often painfully wrong.

For he wasn't really on that dazzling coral beach. He was sealed inside the great metal pear of the trainer, with its flexible effectors caressing every inch of his really naked body. They could numb him with cold, sear him like fire, crush him with pressure.

They often did. The slightest error snatched him away from warm beach and Julie Martinet, into a special mechanical hell where he strove with all his being to earn that supreme reward that was the end of pain.

Sometimes he was trapped aboard a crippled rocket that was falling into the sun. The air was screaming out of the meteor-riddled hull, so that his lungs labored against an agony of suffocation. Cruel light blazed through one jagged hole, blinding, searing, unendurable. The wrecked compartment was a super-heated oven, in which his broken body roasted—but still he heard the voice of Julie Martinet. It came to him faintly through a laser amplifier. Sweetly it sang the combined phonemes of the syllables he had to learn. Sobbing for his breath, he struggled to make each correct response—and he felt the laws of automated learning at work all around him.

When he was wrong, the fire of that devouring sun became instantly more terrible. When his answer was correct, within the narrow limits accepted by the Machine, the searing heat decreased and his struggling lungs found some tiny breath of precious air.

Whenever he got enough answers correct, that nightmare was interrupted. He was back on that dazzling beach with Julie Martinet. She promised him that cooling swim in the surf, or led him toward the tall, cool drinks waiting on a small glass-topped table under the palms, as they began another difficult lesson.

Always, before they reached the glasses or the surf, he had made another error. Each wrong response was instantly inhibited, according to the stern laws of automated learning—though the punishments varied, as if the Machine were experimenting to find what kinds of pain were most effective.

Sometimes he lay sweating in a hospital bed in a floating station in the murky upper air of Venus, gasping for his breath in the thick, hot smog, an infection of the anaerobic parasites eating like acid into his flesh—with Julie's voice cooing monosyllabic Mechanese from his bedside radio.

Sometimes he was pinned by a rockslide in a cave beneath the cold side of Mercury, with a boulder crushing his chest and ice-cold water dripping into his face and great slimy, phosphorescent worms crawling over him, deliberately devouring him—with Julie's voice, near him in the dark, singing the syllables he had to learn.

Always his correct responses were instantly reinforced with some slight reward. Always a sufficient cumulative total of acceptable responses earned him at least a brief relief from pain. When he came back to Julie, she was always sympathetic. Her cool hands caressed him; and bright tears of compassion shone in her eyes.

"Poor dear," she murmured. "I know it's very hard for you. But you must never give up. Just remember what we're striving for. When you've learned enough, you'll receive communion too. We'll be together, then. Let's try another lesson now. If you do well enough, perhaps the Machine will let us take that swim."

He always shivered when she spoke of communion, or when he caught a glimpse of the bright plate in her forehead. He was careful to say nothing about that secret fear, but sometimes he wondered if the Machine, with its sensors against every inch of his body, might not detect it.

For his fear of communion kept growing, like some evil, unearthly weed, until it was more terrible than the synthetic hells that the trainer made to punish his worst errors. It lurked like some hideous hard-scaled pyropod in the shadows of his mind, haunting him until he begged Julie to let him out of the trainer.

She laughed at him.

"Really, you are very lucky," she assured him brightly. "The trainer is a new device. Mechanese was very much harder for me, because I had to learn without it. With the trainer you can't help learning. Just keep trying; you'll reach communion in no time at all."

He didn't dare to tell her that he didn't want communion.

"Truly," she bubbled joyously, "the trainer is the womb of the machine. Inside it you are being mechanized. Your inefficient random human responses are being eliminated. You are learning precision and efficiency and speed. When you are born again, out of the trainer, you will be a perfected child of the Machine."

He tried not to shudder.

"Now let's begin with the nominal structure," she

urged him brightly. "You have already mastered the Machine's basic analysis of the universe as process. Mechanese has no nouns or verbs, but only things-in-process. Remember?"

Afraid of the baking heat in that wrecked ship, the burning fire of that parasitic infection, the gnawing mandibles of those phosphorescent worms, he nodded hastily.

"For example," she trilled, "there is only one basic nominal for any object of solid matter. Such aspects as material, size, shape, and use are indicated by inflection. But it is not a noun, because the verbal intonations always convey the sense of process, so that each possible monosyllabic form is a complete statement."

Her warm smile tantalized him.

"If you study well, perhaps we can take that swim—"

He tried—the third law of mechanized education forced him to try—but they never took the swim.

A time came when Julie vanished. He heard a hiss of air and felt a sudden icy draft against his sweating nakedness.

Back in the training center, he squirmed across the slick pink membrane of the sensor-effector sheath, climbed into his cold coveralls, and scrambled down the flimsy metal ladder.

"Good night, sir." The plump young Techtenant looked bored and sleepy now. "See you next shift, sir."

He wanted terribly never to see the Techtenant or the trainer again, because they meant that he was going to be wired for communion. He wanted desperately to run away—somehow to get back to Quarla Snow and the clean Reefs of Space.

But he was exhausted and guarded and imprisoned . . . he didn't know where . . . perhaps beneath a mile of solid rock . . . perhaps beneath the sea. He did his stint of calisthenics and took a steaming shower and sweated out the chow line and went to his tiny, tile-walled room to sleep.

Suddenly a gong was thundering. It was time to get up, to let them shave his head again, to strip and smear himself with that sticky jelly, to return to the womb of the Machine. . . .

And a time came, in the trainer, when Julie Martinet —or the projected image of her—gave him a test and, smiling, told him that he had passed.

"You have earned communion now. You are ready to be born again."

He almost gasped that he didn't want communion. But he bit his lip. He kept silent until Julie's bright image vanished and air valves roared and a cold wind caught him as he was finally born from the Machine.

Half-dazed and reeling—*Doped!* his mind whispered despairingly to him—he found himself in his cot. He did not know how he got there. He knew only something was wrong: there was some new scent in the atmosphere, some hardly perceived whisper of motion, as if someone were waiting outside his room for him to be asleep.

Then the anesthetic gas that had been piped through his pillow took effect. He slept. Deeply.

When he woke he felt a minor but nagging ache in the skin and the bone of his forehead.. He was in another room—green-walled, surgical.

He did not have to touch his forehead to know that while he slept the surgeons had been at work, the hair-thin electrodes slipped into the micrometrically located centers of his brain, the bright badge of communion implanted on his brow.

In the mammalian brain exist bundles of nerves and specialized tissue which control mood and emotion, as well as those which control motor activities, homeostatic regulation, conscious thought, and the various other activities of that three-pound mass of hypertrophied tissue.

One such area is the pleasure center. Slip a fine platinum electric wire into it by stereotaxic surgery. Feed it a carefully measured, milliampere-tiny surge of electricity. The result is ecstasy! Fit a laboratory animal with such an electrode and with a key it can operate, and it will go on pressing the key, pressing the key, pressing the key . . . it will not pause for food or drink or fear . . . it will sear itself with delight until it collapses of exhaustion, and will awake only to press the key once more.

The jolt of ecstasy that tore through Boysie Gann's being in that first moment of awakening with the communion plate in his forehead and the electrodes embedded in his brain was like nothing he had ever imagined. It was taste, feeling, odor, and light; it was the wild delight of sex and the terrifying joy of daredevil sport; it was all the things he had ever known at once, magnified unbearably. Time stopped.

He was adrift in a turbulent sea of sensation. . . .

Eons and lifetimes later, he became conscious of humanity again. He was back in his body. The tides of quintessential pleasure had receded from around him, and left him aching and dry.

He opened his eyes, and saw a Technicorps medical orderly retreating from him, the communion probe wires in his hand. He had been cut off from the joy of the Planning Machine.

Gann took a long shuddering breath and reconciled himself to being human again. He could understand Sister Delta Four. He could accept his destiny in communion with the Machine. No other reward could be half as great as this, no other purpose as important . . .

Dazedly he became aware that something was wrong. The Technicorps man's face was pale with fear. Voices shouted from outside, and one of them was queerly familiar.

Gann struggled to his feet, apprehensive and wary. When the door burst open, it was Machine General Wheeler who came into the room like a raging typhoon. "Gann!" he roared. "Starchild! You devil, what have you done?"

"I? Done? Nothing, General—and I'm not the Starchild, I swear it!"

"Filth!" howled the general. "Don't lie to me! What have you done to the Planning Machine?"

Gann started to reply, to defend himself. The general gave him no chance. "Lies!" he raged. "Starchild, you've destroyed us all! Admit it! Admit that it was you who has driven the Planning Machine hopelessly mad!"

XII

The Plan of Man had gone amok. All over Earth, out into the asteroid belt, in the refrigerated warrens on Mercury, in the sunless depths of Pluto and on the slowly wheeling forts of the Spacewall, the terror had struck.

Routing orders crashed one subcar ball into another two thousand miles below the surface of the earth. Six hundred persons died in a meteor-like gout of suddenly blazing gases that melted the subcar shaft and let the molten core pour in.

On Venus a Technicaptain received routine programming instructions from the Machine and, obediently, set a dial and turned a switch. It flooded forty thousand hard-won acres of reclaimed land with oily brine.

A "man of golden fire" appeared on the stage of the great Auditorium of the Plan in Peiping, where the Vice-Planner for Asia had been scheduled to speak to his staff. The golden man disappeared again, and twenty raging pyropods flashed out of nowhere into the hall, killing and destroying everything within reach. The Vice-Planner, minutes late in keeping his engagement, had his life spared in consequence.

In short, sharp words, Machine General Wheeler barked out the story of the catastrophes that were overwhelming the Plan. "The Starchild! Seen in the vaults of the Planning Machine—and now the Machine's gone mad. Its orders are wrong! Its data can't be trusted! Gann, if you are the Starchild—"

Boysie Gann had been pushed too far. In a shout louder than Wheeler's own he roared, "General! I'm not the Starchild! Don't be a fool!"

Suddenly the machinelike face of the general seemed to wilt and crack. It was in a very human voice that he said, after a moment. "No. Perhaps you're not. But what in the name of the Plan is going on?"

Gann snapped, "I thought you were telling me that. What's this about the Starchild being seen in the Machine itself?"

"Just that, Gann. Guards reported someone there. A squad was sent down, and they saw him. He was at the manual consoles—changing the settings, erasing miles of tape, reversing connections. The Machine is mad now, Gann. And the Plan is going mad with it. All over the world."

"Never mind that! What did he look like, this Starchild?"

Machine General Wheeler squared his shoulders and barked crisply, "A man. Golden, they say. Almost as if he were luminous. Photographs were taken, but he was not recognized. It . . . didn't resemble you, Gann. But I thought—"

"You thought you'd come here anyway. Use me as a scapegoat, maybe. Is that it? The way you did when you pretended I shot Delta Four?"

The general tried to protest; then his lips smacked shut like the closing of a trap. He nodded his head twice, briskly, like a metronome. "Yes!"

Gann was taken aback. He had not expected so quick a confession. All he could do was say, "But why? Why did you shoot her? To get her out of the way as a witness?"

"Of course," rapped Machine General Wheeler.

"And pretend I was the Starchild? To make yourself more important to the Planner and the Machine?"

"Precisely," the general crackled out.

Gann studied him thoughtfully, then said, "Something must have changed your mind. What was it?"

The general answered without changing expression or tone. Only a faint color on the brow, a pale brightness as of perspiration, showed the strain he must have felt. "The girl recovered," he snapped. "She told the Planner the truth—that I had merely found that document, and planted it on you. The Planner reported to the Machine, and—"

"And what?" demanded Boysie Gann.

The general's voice cracked. "And the Machine went mad. It ordered my arrest. Then it began ordering the arrest of Sister Delta Four, the Vice-Planner for Central America, the guards in the Hall of the Planner, even the Planner himself. There was confusion. I shot my way clear. I secured an aircraft, the one Sister Delta Four had come to the Planner's headquarters in, and I escaped. But I must leave Earth, Gann! I want you to take me to the Reefs, because . . . because I must get away."

"Get away? Why?"

The general's voice tolled out the answer. "In shooting my way out of the Planner's headquarters, I killed two men. One of them was the Planner."

Boysie Gann had never known where the training school was located on Earth. As they emerged to the surface he saw for the first time the great sweep of mountains to the north, felt the icy sting of cold air, and realized that they were on the plateaus below the Himalayas. For thousands of years only nomads and warriors had shared this bleak, desolate land. Now a great hydroelectric plant boomed beyond the level sweep of a rocketport hewn out of rock.

There was something about the power plant that looked strange. As Machine General Wheeler led him quickly to a waiting jetcraft Gann realized what was wrong with the hydroelectric plant. Even at this distance he could see that it was a wreck. Its great windows reflected no light; they were shattered. There were cracks in its solid masonry walls. There had been an explosion within—some mighty burst of short-circuiting energy, volatilizing all matter within its scope.

"Never mind that," rapped out the general. "Come aboard! There's someone there you'll want to see."

Gann followed, staring about. If destruction had come even here, it must be radically more far-reaching than he had dreamed.

Was it the Starchild?

And who was the Starchild? Hurrying after General Wheeler, Gann's mind was a vortex of thoughts, memories, impressions. The body-shaking rupture of his communion with the Machine. The terrible fight in the Planner's hall, and the terrible shock that had struck him when he saw Sister Delta Four—the girl who had once been Julie Martinet, his love—shot down before him. The long, dizzying fall through nonspace, from the Reefs to Earth. The strange hermit, Harry Hickson . . .

It was almost more than he could take in. Bemused, he was hardly aware when they reached the waiting jetship. He followed General Wheeler into the open hatch, and then he saw who it was who awaited them there.

"Julie!" he cried. "Julie Martinet!"

But it was Sister Delta Four who answered. "Come in. Close the hatch. We must take off at once! I have a message from the Machine."

General Wheeler reacted at once. He turned and closed the hatch, then leaped across the narrow cabin of the jetship and snatched from the grasp of Sister Delta Four the black cube that was her linkbox. "Fool!" he rasped. "A message from the Machine! Don't you know the Machine's gone mad? The Starchild has been tampering with it. It is no longer functioning according to Plan. The evidence of your eyes should tell you that. Can't you see what's been going on?"

The girl lifted her head, unafraid, and stared at him with objective, remote eyes. The black fabric of her hood fell away, baring the bright medallion of the communion plate in her forehead, just like Boysie Gann's own. She said in her melodic, chiming voice, "I serve the Machine, General Wheeler. And you are a traitor, condemned to death."

"So are you, for that matter," growled the general. He tossed the linkbox to Boysie Gann. "Here. Keep her quiet while I get us started. We've got to get off Earth at once." He dived for the control cabin to set the automatic instruments that would start the motors, take the plane off the field, fly it straight and true to its destination, radio for landing instructions, and set it down. Gann glanced at the linkbox in his hands, then at Sister Delta Four.

The linkbox carried its communion plug racked in a recess in its cubical bulk. Gann could see the bright glitter of its rounded tips that mated so perfectly with the plate in his own skull.

If, he thought ponderously, he were to take that plug off its clip and place it into the plate in his forehead . . . if he were to complete his communion . . . he would once again feel that total rapture, that almost unbearable ecstasy of soul and senses that he had tasted, just once, an hour before.

The temptation was overpowering.

He could understand Julie—or rather, Sister Delta Four—a great deal better now. There had never been an addiction like this one, no drug, no narcotic, no mere alcoholic craving that was as overpowering in its appeal.

He could understand why Julie Martinet had given up family, freedom, the pleasures of the senses, and himself for the shroud of an acolyte of the Machine.

He could understand it, because he was all but at that point himself, after one single exposure. . . .

With a swift motion, before he could stop to think, he lifted the linkbox and dashed it to the floor. It crackled and sputtered. In its static-filled buzzing sound he could detect some of the tonal morphemes he had been taught, but he did not give himself a chance to puzzle out their meaning, did not allow the linkbox the time to beg for its preservation—if that was its intention. He lifted a foot and crushed it, stamped it again and again, like a noxious insect. Its buzzing abruptly stopped. There was a faint blue flash of electric sparks; then it was only a mangled mass of printed circuits and crushed transistors.

"That's the end of that, Julie," he said. "And that's the end of our relationship with the Machine."

She was watching him silently, her eyes dark and incurious.

"Don't you have anything to say?" he demanded.

She pealed, "Only what I am instructed to tell you, Major Gann. The message that was given me by the Machine."

"Damn the Machine!" he cried. "Can't you understand that's over? It's finished. Gone! First we have to try to straighten out this mess; then—*maybe* then!—we can think about using the Machine again. Using it! Not letting it use us!"

"I know nothing of that, Major Gann," she sang. "I only know the message. It follows: *To Major Gann. Action. Proceed at once to the "Togethership" on the Reefs of Space via Mercury Terminator Line Station Seven. Message ends.*"

Gann shook his head dazedly. "Julie, Julie!" he protested. "That's ridiculous on the face of it. Go to the
Reefs by way of Mercury? That's like coming across a
room by way of . . . of Deneb. It's not the way at all—"

"I don't know about that," rasped the voice of Machine General Wheeler from behind him. Gann turned.
The general was standing in the open door of the control
cabin, something in his hand. His expression was dark
and fearful, like some trapped and dangerous creature of
the jungle.

Gann said, "But Mercury is near the Sun. Even if we
wanted to go to the farthest part of the Reefs, where
we're at superior conjunction, we might go *near* Mercury,
yes, but we'd never land there. Not anywhere on the
planet, much less at some particular station on the terminator line."

"Go there we will," rapped General Wheeler. "Land
there we will. And at the station. Major Gann! I told you
I intended to go to the Reefs at once and wanted you
with me. I had a reason. See here! This dropped to the
ground before me as I was leaving the Planner's chambers after my—ah—episode with the guns."

Wordlessly Boysie Gann took the document. It was a
creamy square, without signature, and on it were the
words:

If you would save yourself, your people, and your
worlds, bring Machine Major Boysie Gann and
yourself to the *Togethership* on the Reefs of Space.
The gateway will be found at the Plan of Man solar
observatory on Mercury, Terminator Station Seven.

"The Starchild!" cried Gann.
General Wheeler nodded with a harsh, mechanical up-
down, up-down.

"A message from the Starchild, yes. And the same message from the Planning Machine. Major Gann! Do you realize what this means? The Planning Machine is the Starchild!"

XIII

At some point they transshipped into a Plan of Man jetless-drive cruiser. Gann paid little attention.

He was using the time in the best way he could, to rest, to try to recover from the shocks and stresses of the last few weeks. And how fast they had accumulated, how violently they had drained him of strength, and of peace of mind!

He could still feel the distant ache in his forehead, in the bones of his skull, behind his eyes, in his sinuses —the track of the probes of the surgeons who had implanted the communion electrodes in his brain.

He could feel the aches and bruises of his working over by the Planner's guards. How long ago?

He was exhausted still from the battle with the pyropods and the long drop to Earth. His weary muscles still bore the fatigue poisons of his fight on Harry Hickson's reeflet . . .

He closed his eyes, and Quarla Snow came into his mind. He opened them, and Sister Delta Four sat quietly unmoving, her eyes fixed on him, before him.

He was beginning to feel himself again. With the return of strength there returned the question of the two women, so unlike yet so much in his thoughts. He said, "Julie. Sister Delta Four, if you'd rather. Do you know that what General Wheeler said is true? That the Machine is mad?"

Her perfect face, half hidden in the cowl, did not change expression. "I know that is what the general said," she sang.

"But it is mad, Julie. The Starchild has wrecked it. Now it is wrecking the Plan planets. Do you still want to serve it?"

"I serve the Planning Machine," she chimed sweetly, her dark eyes cool and empty.

"Because of the bliss of communion? I understand that, Julie. Don't forget"—he touched the glittering plate in his forehead—"I've felt it too."

There was a flicker in her eyes, almost an expression of indulgent amusement as she looked at him. But she only said, in her voice like the sound of bells, "What you felt, Major Gann, is only a shabby imitation of what the Machine gives its true servants. For you are only half a servant. The Machine has not opened its mind to you."

Puzzled, Gann asked, "You mean . . . mind-to-mind linkage? Communication with the—what could you call it?—with the *thoughts* of the Machine?"

She only shrugged. "It is something of that sort, perhaps," she said indifferently. "You cannot know." She sang a quick chiming chorus of tonal morphemes. Gann tried to follow, but was lost almost at once.

"You said something about the . . . the *soul?*" he guessed. "The soul of the Machine?"

"You see? I am sorry for you, Major Gann," she said. "More for you than for myself. Since you have destroyed my linkbox I cannot reach the Machine, but some day perhaps I will find another linkbox. You will never attain it."

Machine General Wheeler had been dozing while they spoke. Now Gann became aware that the general was awake and listening to them. When he saw Gann's eyes on him, the general sat up and laughed raspingly, like an ancient, ill-kept machine.

"A fool," he said, hurling one bright, contemptuous look at the girl. "And you're another, Gann. You're not fit to survive, either of you."

"I survive if the Machine desires it," chimed the girl clearly. "I will cease when the Machine no longer needs me."

The general ticked off a nod and turned to Gann. "You see? And what is it that keeps you alive?"

Gann said seriously, "I don't know." He got up, moved restlessly about the cramped quarters of the Plan cruiser, his step light and imprecise in the tiny gravity its jetless thrust supplied. He said, "Out on the Reefs they talk about freedom. I'm not sure, but . . . Yes. I think it is that hope that keeps me going now, the hope that freedom is real, and good."

The general laughed again. Without passion, as if playing back an ancient tape recording in his brain, he said, "The Planner I just killed understood freedom. He called it 'the romantic fallacy.' Freedom is what permits the dirty, Planless nomads of the Reefs to eke out their wretched lives. It is a myth."

"I saw happy men and women on the Reefs," said Boysie Gann softly, less to the general than to himself.

"You saw animals! They believe that men are good. They believe that mere human men and women, left to their own un-Planned devices on any drifting rock somewhere in space, can somehow find within themselves the natural springs of morality and intellectual enlightenment and progress. They are wrong!"

He blinked at Gann and the silent, composed girl. "Men are evil," he said. "The givers of laws have always known that men are essentially bad. They must be goaded into whatever good they display. Our Plan of Man was created to defend this classic philosophy—the cornerstone of all civilization. The Plan recognizes the evil in man. It forces him to goodness and progress. There is no other way!"

Mercury, the hell planet, lay before them.

The guiding sensors of their Plan cruiser reached out with fingers of radiation to touch the planet, the Sun; sought reference points by optical examination of the fixed bright stars; scanned the limbs and poles of Mercury, and accurately fixed the proper point on the terminator line of the sun's radiation. Then, satisfied, or in whatever state passes in a machine for satisfaction, it completed its landing corrections and directed the cruiser into a landing orbit.

The great naked fire of the Sun hung only thirty-odd million miles away—three times as close as to Earth, its mighty outpouring of light and heat nine times as great. Its surface was mottled with great ugly spots, leprous with the scaly markings called faculae and granulations. It was painful to watch, bright and blinding. Machine General Wheeler moved a hand angrily, and the vision screen obediently blotted out the central disk, like a solar eclipse; then they could see the somber scarlet chromosphere, the leaping red arches of prominences, like slow-motion snakes striking at the void and, surrounding all, the white blazing radiance of the corona.

In that mighty furnace, each second, lakes of solar hydrogen flashed into helium, pouring out energy. Each second, every square centimeter of its enormous surface hurled six thousand watts of power into the void.

On the sunward side of Mercury, molten tin and lead ran like water in fissures of baked and ovenlike rock. On its dark side the thinnest of atmospheres, boiled from the rock by the solar radiation, smashed free of it by the impact of meteorites, carried some tiny warmth to relieve what was otherwise a freezing cold nearly as absolute as that of Pluto.

On the terminator line the Plan of Man's string of observatories maintained a precarious existence, the searing heat before them, the killing cold behind.

"There!" rasped General Wheeler, stabbing a finger at the screen. "Terminator Line Station Seven! Now we'll see about this Starchild!"

The great Plan cruiser, dancing in the thrust of its reactionless motors, slowed, halted, kissed the seared rock, and came to rest in the shadow of a silvery dome that reached out toward the sun with the barrels of telescopes and pyrometers, stared toward it with the great blind eyes of radio telescopes and masers. Over its entrance blazed the sign:

THE MIGHTIEST REWARDS
THE MOST FAITHFUL

General Wheeler laughed sharply. "Faithful to whom, eh? To me, Gann! Trust in me!"

Boysie Gann glanced at him without expression, then at Sister Delta Four. She was mute and uncaring, her eyes hidden in the folds of her dark cowl. Gann shook his head but said nothing. In his heart he thought: *Mad. He's as mad as the Machine.*

Tubular entranceways were groping slowly toward them from the dome, found the airlocks of the cruiser, met and sealed themselves.

The hatches opened.

Gann stood up. "Let's go. All of us. I . . . I don't know what we'll find."

He waited and General Wheeler stalked past him, elbows and knees stiff as the linkages of a reciprocating engine. Sister Delta Four approached the lock, then hesitated and looked at Gann.

She threw a series of tonal symbols at him, her voice crisp and pure as bells.

Gann said hesitantly, "I . . . I don't understand. As you said, I'm only about half educated. Something about a . . . a man? A relative?"

Sister Delta Four said in English, "I asked you to be careful, Major Gann. There is a brother here who is of unstable emotion."

"I don't understand," said Boysie Gann. The girl did not answer, only nodded remotely and passed on into the entranceway, into Terminator Station Seven.

As Gann followed her he heard General Wheeler's rasping roar, "Hello there! Anyone! Isn't anyone here?"

The general was standing atop an enameled steel desk, peering around in all directions. Behind him were banks of electronic instruments, arranged in long rows like lockers in a gymnasium; they purred and hummed and flashed with lights, ignoring the presence of the general. The desk itself was part of a small office suite. It was deserted.

"I don't understand," rapped the general. He climbed down, picked up a phone from a desk, and stabbed circuit buttons at random, listened briefly, then flung it down.

"There's no one here," he said, brows gathered in irritation and anger. "A joke? Would this Starchild dare joke with *me*?"

Gann said, "What about the rest of the station, General?"

"Search it!" barked the general. "You too, Sister! There must be someone! The doorway to the Reefs—the key to the *Togethership*—I will not let them escape me!"

Gann looked forebodingly at Sister Delta Four, but she did not return his gaze. Obediently, her fingers telling her sonic beads, she chose a doorway and entered it, her dark cowl moving as she scanned the rooms beyond for signs of life. Gann shrugged and selected an area of his own and began the search.

He could hear General Wheeler's angry shouts, and the purr or whine or click of the automatic machinery of the observatory, keeping its instruments pointed at selected areas of the Sun, tabulating the results. He could hear the distant whine of pumps, the sigh of air in the vents. There were no other sounds. The observatory seemed to be deserted. Gann moved through a chamber of record storage, where stacked drawers of magnetic tape reels held the information gleaned from countless machine-hours of solar study, glanced into what might have been a recreation room, found himself in the main observation chamber.

No one moved. No voice challenged him.

"Hello!" he cried, echoing General Wheeler's fading voice. There was no answer.

The normal complement of a nearly automatic station like this one was small—half a dozen men, perhaps even fewer. Yet it was hard to believe that some disaster had overtaken them all at once . . .

Or so Gann thought.

Then, turning, he saw the disaster.

There were three of them—three men, piled like jackstraws behind a work desk, before a closed and locked door. They were unmistakably dead.

The one on top, supine, sightless yellowed eyes staring at the ceiling, was a grizzled older man in the uniform of a Technicaptain. Of the other two Gann could tell little except for their insignia—a Techtenant and a cadet, one plump and young, one young and oddly familiar.

Gann bent and touched them. There was no pulse. No breath. Yet the bodies still seemed to be warm.

Perhaps it was only his imagination, he thought. Or the warmth of the room—cooled by the circulating refrigerated air from the pumps, yet still so close to the blazing Sun.

He heard a faint sound, and jerked his head up, frowning, listening.

It was not one sound. There were two. One he identified—the faint tones of Sister Delta Four's sonic beads. In her own search of the dome, by some other route, she was coming near.

But what was the other sound? It seemed to come from nearby, though muffled. He turned his head and stared at the locked door. Could it be from behind that? It seemed to be a sort of closet or record-storage chamber. It was massive, and the locks that held it would not respond to any unauthorized key. Yet now he was sure of it: there were sounds behind it, sounds like the distant murmur of life.

Sister Delta Four entered the room, saw him, hurried over to stoop swiftly over the three bodies.

When she looked up her eyes were dark. She sang. "You need not fear him after all, Major Gann."

Boysie Gann blinked. "Fear whom?"

"The brother," the girl intoned. "He is dead. His unPlanned emotions need not concern you any longer."

"Brother? But—" Then Gann stopped in mid-sentence. Understanding began to reach him. He reached for the body of the Technicadet, turned the flaccid head. The face was one he had seen before.

"*Your* brother!" he cried.

Sister Delta Four corrected him. "The brother of Julie Martinet. The brother of this body, yes. As you see, he is dead." Her dark eyes were mild and unconcerned, as if she were commenting on the weather.

Beyond the jackstraw heap of bodies the thick square door still hid the source of the tiny sounds, but Gann put them out of his mind. Julie Martinet's brother! He could see the resemblance, the same grave eyes, the same shape of the jaw . . . In Sister Delta Four, it completed a perfect oval; in the boy it gave him a strong chin under a dreamer's face.

Boysie Gann saw that, and he saw something more. He bent close, incredulous. But there was no doubt. Under the pallor of death, under the uncaring vacancy of the face, there was a hint of color. Golden color. Almost luminous.

Gann turned quickly to the other corpses. The same!

Like Machine Colonel Zafar, like Harry Hickson, like the beasts of the Reefs, the three dead Technicorps men gleamed faintly, goldenly, like a brass helmet's reflection of a distant sun.

He drew Sister Delta Four after him and sought and found General Wheeler, told him in short sentences what he had seen.

"The same golden color, General," he said. "It's fatal. Or . . ." He hesitated, remembering. Harry Hickson had died of the disease, yes. But he had lived again.

He brushed that thought out of his mind. "Fatal," he repeated. "It's a fusorian infection, I think. If you put a drop of their blood under a microscope you would see little fusorian globules, flickering with golden light. Some sort of symbiosis, Dr. Snow said. But fatal . . ."

General Wheeler rasped, "Fusorian, you say? The Reefs, then! Do you know what that means to me, Gann? It means the Starchild! My information was not wrong. He's here!"

"But he can't be," Gann protested. "We've searched the station, the three of us, and we saw no one."

And Sister Delta Four echoed him, "We saw no one, General. No one at all but the dead."

"Dead or alive, he's here," growled the general. "I'll find him! I'll make him lead me to the *Togethership!*"

Boysie Gann remembered the sounds behind the door.

He said, "There is one place, General. One place where
. . . someone might be. Behind the bodies was a door—"

"Come on!" shouted Wheeler, not waiting to hear him
out, and led the way like an animated machine, arms
flailing, harsh breath rasping. Gann and the girl had
found him far from the observatory room, down in the
subterranean storage spaces of the dome, poking and
shouting into recesses of canned food and unused spools
of tape. Even in Mercury's light grasp it was a long,
hard, running climb back to the instrument room, and
even Sister Delta Four was gasping for breath before they
made half the distance back. Then they all stopped, pant-
ing, staring at each other. For all of them had caught
the same sound—the distant rumble of caterpillar tracks,
carried faintly through Mercury's rock and the structure
of the station.

It was the entranceways, the long tubular protuberances
through which their ship had been linked to the lock of
the observatory dome. They were in motion. Either another ship had arrived . . .

Or their own ship was taking off!

"Let's go!" cried Boysie Gann, and they ran the re-
maining distance faster than before.

The great door was standing open and the bodies were
gone.

General Wheeler and Gann turned without words and
searched the room, under desks, behind cabinets, even
inside the servicing hatches of the instruments themselves.
"They're gone," said Gann at last, and the general echoed
his words: "They're gone."

Another voice said, "They've taken your ship, too."

Gann and the general spun around. Sister Delta Four
had not troubled to search the room with them. She had
gone through the door, into a tiny, steel-walled cubicle
that had evidently been designed for holding the most important records in safety in the event of some disaster or

mischance to the station. What it held now was another sort of treasure entirely. It was a girl, her lips white where they had been gagged, her arms still trailing ropes that Sister Delta Four had not finished taking off her. "They took your ship," she repeated. "All three of them. They opened the door for me—and left."

Gann hardly heard what she was saying. Something else was filling his mind. Honey-haired, softly tanned of skin, eyes blue and bright . . . he knew that girl.

The girl in the observation dome in Mercury was the girl he had left weeks and billions of miles from here and now. It was Quarla Snow.

XIV

In the bright, refrigerated dome the pumps poured cooling air in upon them, but the great storm-racked globe of the Sun that hung in the viewing screen seemed to beat down on them as if they were naked on Mercury's rock.

Quarla Snow reached out and touched Boysie Gann's arm. "I thought you were dead," she said wonderingly, and her eyes went toward Sister Delta Four, kneeling beside her, patiently, absently rubbing Quarla's chafed wrists.

"Never mind that," said Gann. "How did you get here? Was it—the Starchild?"

Quarla shook her head, not in denial but in doubt. "I don't know. After you disappeared I set out to look for you."

General Wheeler, at one of the optical telescopes, rapped angrily, "There! I see the villains! Between us and the Sun!" He studied the controls of his instruments furiously, selected a switch and turned it. The great image of the Sun in the screen danced and dwindled as the field of vision of a new telescope replaced the old one.

They saw the Plan cruiser that had brought them, already very remote in the black, star-sprinkled sky that surrounded the blazing globe.

"I wonder who's piloting it," murmured Boysie Gann.

"Those criminals you saw here!" Wheeler barked. "Playing possum! They fooled you! Now they've taken our ship and we're marooned."

"General," said Boysie Gann earnestly, "I don't ask you to believe me, but I was not fooled. They were not pretending to be dead. They were dead."

"Impossible," rasped the general. "Look at the idiots! They're heading straight for the Sun. The ship isn't designed for photosphere temperatures! They'll kill themselves!"

Gann turned wearily back to Quarla Snow. "You said you went looking for me. Why?"

She flushed and looked away. She did not answer the question. She said, "Colonel Zafar died. My father reported it—it was dangerous, you see—and he took the body into Freehaven for examination. He did not know what had become of you. Neither did I. But . . . I thought I could find you."

Sister Delta Four got up quietly, crossed to the girl's other side, began to rub circulation into the other wrist. Quarla went on, her eyes avoiding Boysie Gann's. As she spoke she looked sometimes at Sister Delta Four, sometimes at General Wheeler, sometimes at the great hanging orb of the Sun and the Plan cruiser that was moving slowly toward its long, tentacle-like prominences.

She had gone outside, she said, and called her spaceling. Then she brought Harry Hickson's pyropod out into the open air, released it, watched it circle them twice, then arrow off into space itself . . . and, riding the spaceling, she had followed it.

"After you disappeared and Colonel Zafar died, it seemed to go crazy," she said. "Raced around the house —I thought it was looking for you. And I thought it might find you, if I set it free."

"The Starchild!" boomed General Wheeler. "Get to

the Starchild, woman! Did you ever find the Starchild?"

She hesitated. "I think I did," she said at last. "I think I met the Starchild in the heart of Reef Whirlpool."

Reef Whirlpool—not a planet, not a sun, not a comet. Not even a Reef in the true sense. It was something that partook of some of the elements of all of them. It had begun as a Reef, no doubt. It orbited Sol like a planet, if a distant one; like a comet, most of its bulk was gases. And it burned with hydrogen-helium fusion at its core, like a star.

Basically Reef Whirlpool was simply a bigger, denser cluster of Reefs than most of those stepchildren of Sol. Given time and additions enough, it might some day become the heart of a star.

Its angular momentum was enormous; some stronger force than gravity kept its parts from flying into space. The Reefs that composed it were older and . . . stranger than those outside. Pyropods in queerly mutated forms swarmed in and around it. Its central portions had never been visited by man, not even by the explorers of the Reefs.

It was a place of terror and legend. The life that it harbored had been a long time evolving.

Straight as an arrow the baby pyropod that once had belonged to Harry Hickson hurtled toward Reef Whirlpool—and behind it pursuing, barely able to keep its glowing blue-white trail in sight, followed Quarla Snow on her spaceling.

"I was afraid," she said soberly. "We passed a mating swarm of pyropods. Then ten thousand of them together, wheeling in space in a single body. If they had seen us and pursued we wouldn't have had a chance. But it was too late to worry about that . . . and I was even more afraid of Reef Whirlpool."

"The Starchild, girl!" cried General Wheeler. "Now!"

His eyes were fixed angrily on the screen, where the Plan cruiser was coming closer and closer to the Sun, one great curved prominence seeming almost to lick up toward it like a reaching tongue of flame.

"We reached Reef Whirlpool," said the girl, "and there I lost Hickson's pyropod. But Bella—that's my spaceling —Bella seemed to know where he had gone. We went in."

From nearby in space, Reef Whirlpool looked like a tiny galaxy, its separate reeflets glowing each with its own hue, like bright, soft stars against the dark. The rim of the disk was dark—dead rocks and fragments. There, Quarla thought, were the nesting places of the pyropod swarms. She could feel the spaceling shudder, its limpid eyes wide and glazed with fear. But it went on.

"Bella didn't seem able to help herself," said Quarla Snow. "She seemed to want to go right on—to her own destruction—or to something she feared even more."

"Like those fools in my ship," rapped General Wheeler. "Is that where the Starchild was? In that Reef?"

Quarla Snow hesitated. "I don't know. Truly, General Wheeler, I don't know what I saw in the Reef. I know that I saw a great many things that weren't there."

"Illusions?" the general demanded. "You were hallucinating?"

She nodded uncertainly. "Yes . . . No. I don't know. I only know I saw things that couldn't have been there. One of them was Harry Hickson, and I knew he was dead. Another was Colonel Zafar. And another—why, Boysie, one of them was you."

They were deep in the core of Reef Whirlpool now. The spaceling's frenzy grew. They were long past the outer rim of rock where the pyropods nested, but there was something ahead that terrified Bella more than the tunneled nests of the beasts.

"It's all right, honey," said the voice of her father in her ear.

She cried out and stared around her. He was not there. No one was there, inside the tiny envelope of air the spaceling carried with them as they fled through dead, airless space.

"Go on, darling," said another voice. It was the voice of the man she had just seen disappear in a whirlpool of light, the man she was seeking, Boysie Gann.

And a third voice: "Quarla, girl! Don't hang back now!" And that was the voice that terrified her most of all, for she knew it, though she had not heard it in a long time and knew its owner was dead. It was the voice of Harry Hickson.

Illusion?

It had to be illusion. Hickson was dead. No one was there—no one in sight, and no possibility that someone could be lurking out of sight, beyond Bella's envelope of air. For outside that elastic sphere there was nothing to carry a voice's sound.

Yet that illusion stayed with her. "Don't fret about pyropods, girl," advised the voice, slow, rough, kind —Harry Hickson's own, she was sure of it. "Get on with it! We're waiting for you."

She remembered some words the dying Colonel Zafar had said: ". . . mind trap . . . beware your heart's desire . . ." There was a warning there.

But she could not take caution from the warning; will she, nill she, the spaceling was carrying her deeper and deeper into Reef Whirlpool, with the gleam of lesser reeflets darting past them as they flew, glittering diamond fungi, luminous blue polygons, jungles of incandescent wire, glowing nightmare worldlets for which she could find no name.

And then they were at what she knew was the core.

A great ship swung emptily about, huge as the whole

Reef of Freehaven, giant, lethal weapons staring out of open ports. It was in free orbit at the heart of Reef Whirlpool. Its weapons were unmanned. Its drives were silent.

"Great Plan!" shouted Machine General Wheeler, wild with excitement. "The *Togethership!* It had to be the *Togethership!*"

Quarla Snow looked at him, faintly puzzled. "That was the name it bore, yes. Your ship, General?"

The general cackled with glee. "It is now! My ship—my Machine that's been locked in its holds—and my worlds, as soon as I reach it! You'll take me there, woman. You'll lead me to the *Togethership!* When I've made myself the master of the Planning Machine it carries I'll be back here on the Plan Worlds. Not just a general—not even a Planner—I'll rule the Machine itself! I'll—" He broke off, staring at Boysie Gann. "What's the matter?" he rapped.

Gann said, "How do you propose to reach it, General?"

The general's face darkened. He scowled at the screen, where his cruiser, now hopelessly beyond his reach, seemed to be dodging around the great solar flare that had developed in the moments while they were watching.

"Go on," he growled. "I'll find a way. I'll get the *Togethership,* and then . . . Never mind! Go on."

Around that great battlecraft of the Plan, painted dead black for camouflage in space, studded with laser scopes and bristling with missile launchers, there was a queer golden mist.

Quarla looked, and looked again. It was like a fog of liquid gold. Like a golden cloud.

Impossible that there should be a cloud in space, even here. Yet she saw it. And at its heart was a great golden sphere, larger and brighter than the elfin Reefs, more perfectly round.

Like a laser burst hurtling to a target, the spaceling drove toward it. Quarla cried out in terror, for as they raced toward it its surface seemed to lift to meet them. A bulge appeared and grew, became a tentacle reaching toward them. And the phantom voice of Harry Hickson said roughly, "Quarla, honey! Don't be scared. Come on!"

She could not have stopped if she had tried. Bella was out of control.

The voice was surely illusion, yet Quarla found it reassuring. Her horror ebbed. Queerly detached, she watched the bulge on the golden surface swell and divide into three parts. Each stretched out until it became a bright golden snake. She watched them coil toward her . . .

They struck.

Hot yellow coils whipped and tightened around her.

Yet there was no pain. There was even less fear. The living ropes of gold hauled her in like a hooked trout, down to that golden sphere, and her calm and detachment grew. Even the spaceling had lost all of its fear. Nestling into the hot, contracting coils, Bella purred like a huge kitten. She was drowsy.

Quarla was drowsy too. She thought she heard Harry Hickson speaking to her again—calmly but urgently—telling her things of great importance. *You must go, child,* he seemed to say, *you must go to this place and do that thing. You must avoid these. Then you must return here* . . .

It was greatly soothing to hear his calm, wise voice. Quarla Snow slept.

She slept, and time passed. . . .

"And," she said, "when I woke up, I knew what I must do. I had to come here and fetch you. All of you. He wants you to come to him."

General Wheeler rasped, "The Starchild! He's the one you mean, eh?"

But she was shaking her head obstinately. "I don't know that. I only know what I must do. Only"—her expression became worried—"the men were here and they were afraid of me. They locked me up. They would not listen."

Sister Delta Four sang, "Major Gann. General Wheeler. Miss Snow. Have you observed the screen?"

They turned as one, startled, staring at the screen.

Up there hung the Sun. The bright prominence that had grown so swiftly was huger still. It overhung the shape of the fleeing Plan cruiser with the three men who should have been dead—overhung it like a crested wave, like the hood of a striking cobra.

And like a snake it was striking.

The Plan cruiser had changed direction—too late. Slow though the great, jetting tongue of flame seemed in the screen, its movement was miles per second. Twist and turn though it would, the cruiser could not escape. The prominence touched it.

The tiny black shape disappeared.

Boysie Gann found himself shaking, heard the metallic, monotonous steady cursing of the general by his side. The cruiser had been swept out of space. Slowly the incredible tongue of flame began to fall back toward the mottled surface of its star, the Sun.

The general recovered himself first. The coppery spikes of his hair, his flat bronze features, his whole expression showed resolution. "All right," he said. "We don't have to worry about trying to get that ship back any more. It's gone. Question is, how do we get out of here? Second question, how do we then get to the Reefs—and the *Togethership?*"

Sister Delta Four sang proudly, "There will be no

difficulty in that. The Machine has said that the gateway to the *Togethership* is to be found here."

The general fixed his steel-gray stare on her. "But where? Out that airlock? Onto the rock of dayside Mercury? We'd fry in minutes. Or do you suggest we fly?"

He stopped in mid-sentence, bronze face frozen, then turned on Quarla Snow. "Those beasts of yours! What became of them? The spacelings, or whatever you called them."

But Quarla was shaking her head. "This near the Sun, Bella would never live," she said. "The radiation would destroy her—and us, too, if we were in her air capsule. And anyway, she's not here."

"Then how?" cried the general. "There must be a way! Both messages—the Starchild's and the Machine's—they both said this was the way."

Quarla said softly, "And so it is, General. That is why I came here, to fetch you to the Reefs. I don't know how. I only know it will happen."

The room seemed to lurch.

It caught all of them off guard. They turned to look at each other with varying expressions of surprise and fear.

"I think," said Boysie Gann grimly, "that we've found our gateway." He knew that sensation, had felt it before, knew that in the powers it involved the long climb outward to the orbits of the Reefs was only a matter of moments.

He was not afraid. In fact, there was almost relief in the knowledge that soon they would be facing the presence that had dislocated a solar system. Yet something was troubling him, some question of the last few moments, something that had been asked but not answered.

He felt the room lurch again, and the lights grew distant and dim. Then he remembered.

"Why, Quarla?" he croaked hoarsely.

The girl of the Reefs looked at him affectionately. "Why what, Boysie?"

"Why were they afraid of you? You said the men here feared you. *Why?*"

The room seemed to shake and twist itself, as if viewed through a defective glass. The lights were leaving them—or they the lights, as if new quanta of space were being born between them, separating them without motion like the recession of fleeing galaxies.

And then Gann saw the answer. Quarla did not need to speak. His eyes told him what had terrified the three men in Terminator Station Seven.

In the dwindling light Quarla alone stood forth bright and clear—her face, her arms, her body shining brightly . . .

With a golden glow.

XV

They tumbled through space endlessly and forever, and then they stopped.

They had arrived. They were all together in a wondrous new world.

All about them hung the slowly spinning worldlets of Reef Whirlpool, jewels of emerald and ruby, glowing gems of white light and blue. There was the slowly pulsing golden sphere that had captured Quarla Snow. And there the great battleship of the Plan, the *Togethership*.

Quarla Snow had described the ship, but she had not made them see its immensity. The vessel was huge.

Boysie Gann saw it, and saw too that they were not alone.

A ton of rushing mass hurtled toward them and stopped in midflight, squealing happily. A glowing red nose nuzzled Quarla Snow. "Bella!" cried the girl, and patted the tawny velvet fur. She murmured to Gann, "My spaceling. We're in her envelope of air, you see. Without it we'd not live a minute here."

General Wheeler rapped, "Get your sentimental reunion over with, woman! Can this beast take us to the *Togethership?*"

"We're going there now," said Quarla Snow. "See for yourself, General."

They were. Gann could it now, see the great battlecraft growing as they drew close. They were in free fall within the spaceling's vital capsule, all four of them in loose and tumbling attitudes, Quarla with one hand on the spaceling's coat, Sister Delta Four, proud and dignified even in the sprawl of zero-G, Machine General Wheeler, careless of everything around him but his goal, his steel-gray eyes fixed on the looming *Togethership*.

The battlecraft of the Plan was more distant and more immense even than Gann had realized. It grew into a long planetoid of sleek black metal, hanging suspended in the space between the glowing golden sphere that dominated Reef Whirlpool's core and the tumbling worldlets that brightened the sky about them. The four circled it and found the valves of a lock yawning open at its base, circled by the jutting black cylinders of the six great drive units that had thrust it up from Earth.

It did not seem to have been used in all those years. It had an abandoned and empty look.

The spaceling, without direction, seeming compelled by some outside force, took them straight into those valves, and halted.

The entry port of the *Togethership* was as big as a three-story house. As they entered, luminous rings around its walls sprang into soft gray light. The great valves moved silently, remorselessly shut behind them.

They were enclosed in a wall of steel.

All around them the walls were pitted and scarred, as if from some enormous battle of the past. There had been no such battle, Gann knew. What could have done it? Could it have been meteorites, over the decades that the locks had hung open?

General Wheeler saw his look and rapped, "Pyropods! They've been chewing at my ship! By the Plan, I'll root out every filthy one of them—"

The general was right, Gann realized. Not only right, but seething with anger. It had become *his ship*, containing *his* copy of the Planning Machine. And with it he intended to make all the worlds of the solar system *his* planets. . . .

Darkly, Boysie Gann realized that there were more dangerous things in this ship than pyropods.

He became aware of a sighing, rustling noise, and saw that the lock was filling with air. The spaceling's vital capsule no longer protected them from the void; they were in a breathable atmosphere. The spaceling realized it even before he did. She flicked her seal-like tail and darted away; raced back, her red nose glowing with joy, whimpering with pleasure. She played games with the bright-leafed vines she had carried in her air-envelope—the curious Reef plants that were part of the elaborate evolutionary device that enabled a warm-blooded oxygen-breather like herself to survive in naked space. She rolled the waxy, luminous tendrils into a huge ball, tossed it with her glowing nose, chased it across the lock, caught it with her broad velvet tail . . .

"Bella!" called Quarla Snow, affectionately stern. "Come back here! Behave yourself!"

But the spaceling was playfully obstinate. She flashed across the lock and back, racing toward them like the charge of a pyropod, missed them by inches, returned to the inner wall—and there, at the far end of the lock, discovered a crevice that had not been there seconds before. Mewing excitedly, the spaceling slid its supple body through the narrow opening and was gone.

A way was open into the rest of the ship. The same machinery that had turned on the lights and closed the outer valves had now opened a passage inside.

"Hah!" shouted General Wheeler. "At last! The Machine is waiting for me!" And he was gone almost as rapidly as the spaceling.

More slowly, the others followed—Quarla Snow, on the track of her pet, Boysie Gann, Sister Delta Four, a somber figure in black at the rear of the procession. A pseudo-gravity field of a tenth of a G or so gave them footing but spared them much of the effort of moving their bodies up the winding shafts from the lock. Even so, Gann was winded trying to keep up with the racing, driving general.

They were in a shaft seeming to extend endlessly upward. Then they passed a point of change-of-thrust of the pseudo-gravity and it became a dizzy abyss into which they were falling, until their protesting bodies oriented themselves to the new kinesthetic sensations and accepted it as a level hall. A cold current came along it, setting them to shivering, a breeze out of a cave, with a faintly unpleasant reek, dusty and bitter and dry.

A faint murmuring vibration was borne by the air current along the tube.

Quarla Snow moved closer to Boysie Gann. Unconsciously he touched her shoulder, hurried past her. Whatever the sound was, it could wait.

The general was out of sight.

Gann stepped up his pace, gasping for breath. The air was thinner here than he was used to, as if the old refresher tanks were running dry. He glanced around and found himself at a numbered landing, where the gray light faintly showed a sign, MESS C.

Long tables stretched off into darkness, where crewmen in flight must have stood to eat their meals.

Gann stopped and waited for the girls to catch up with him. "The general's gone," he said. "After his Planning Machine. I . . . I think he may find it, and I'm afraid of what may happen if he does." He glanced at Quarla, the concern on her face caused mostly by worry about her vanished spaceling, and at Sister Delta Four, whose hooded eyes showed no expression at all. He said, "If the Machine on this ship is half as powerful as the one on Earth—and they say it is more than that, an exact duplicate—then Wheeler just might rule the solar system with it."

Quarla Snow said only, "What do you want us to do?"

"Split up. Find him. He's armed, of course. Don't try to handle him yourself, either of you. Just scream—good and loud—so I can find you."

Sister Delta Four's pure, chiming voice was like a breath of reason. "You are not armed either, Major Gann. You will be no more able to cope with him than we."

"Let me worry about that! Just find him if you can . . . What's the matter?"

"Nothing is the matter, Major Gann," said Sister Delta Four, her face still hooded.

"Not you. Quarla. What is it?"

Quarla said unhappily, "It . . . it can't be dangerous, Boysie. I mean, you don't have to worry."

Gann laughed sharply, unable to help himself; her reassurance was so pathetically out of place.

"No, I mean it, Boysie. After all, we're not here by accident. I was sent to bring you. All of you. The . . . the Starchild, if that's who it was that sent me—he'll know how to handle the general."

"I don't intend to take that chance," said Gann grimly. "Quarla, go on down the passage, Julie, follow her, check all the side ways. I'll look around here and follow."

He was halfway through the ancient mess hall and the girls out of sight before he realized something.

She didn't correct me when I called her Julie, he thought. And wondered why.

Gann found himself shaking as he followed the polished guiderails between the endless rows of long, high tables —not with fear but exhaustion. Exhaustion and something else.

The more fatigue tried to slow him down, the more it weakened his control, the more he remembered that one incredible moment-long lifetime of ecstasy the Machine had given him in those last few minutes before it had gone mad. The longing was almost physical. He understood Sister Delta Four's addiction. She must be suffering far more than he—her addiction longer standing, and if what she had said was true, at a far higher pitch. Perhaps that was why she had seemed strained. . . . And Quarla Snow. The girl was sick! That golden glow had meant death to Machine Colonel Zafar and to the three in the Mercury observatory . . . death, or something far more terrifying than death.

He forced his mind away from both girls and onto his quest. It was vitally important to find the general. Gann cursed himself for not having anticipated the problem. Yet there was little he could have done; when all was said and done, the general had had the arms, not he. Not that the general needed them as far as Gann was concerned, not as long as he wore the security collar. He touched it absently. Freedom . . . a world without collars . . . a world where men could live like men, not like the Machine's cogs . . .

He jerked his hand away, appalled.

He realized he had been wandering among these benches for minutes! What was the matter with him? Why was his mind wool-gathering?

It could be fatigue, he thought. *Or hunger.* He glanced around; he was in the galley for Mess C. But no drop flowed when he tried the taps at the sinks. The pantries and lockers gave him no more. Neat labels on bins named the foods they should have contained, but every bin was empty.

No matter. Boysie Gann pushed that thought out of his mind, too, and resumed his search.

Mess B and Mess A were equally spotless and equally bare. There was nothing else on that level.

The level above was crew quarters, emptied and abandoned. No doubt Quarla or Sister Delta Four had already searched them; Gann hurried on, back into the queer gravitational inversion of the passage, to the next level. The distant mutter of sound was louder now, but he still could not identify it . . .

Until he saw the landing where a locked door greeted him with the sign, RESTRICTED TO MACHINE PERSONNEL.

Behind those locked steel doors was the muffled and multitudinous humming vibration. The lost slave unit of the Planning Machine. Still running.

Or running again? Had General Wheeler reached it, started it up? And what was it planning now?

Boysie Gann hammered on the door. "You, inside there!" he bawled. "Open up! Let me in!"

Only the dulled mechanical mumble answered him.

"Open!" he roared. "I know you're in there, General Wheeler!"

A great chuckling laugh sounded in his ear. "Not at all, Major Gann," boomed the voice of the Planner.

Gann whirled. The Planner here?

No one was in sight.

"You might as well keep going, Boysie," advised the voice of Technicadet M'Buna in a tone of friendly concern. "You're wasting time, you know."

Gann stood paralyzed. But M'Buna was dead! And so, he remembered tardily, was the old Planner; General Wheeler had shot him down. "Who's there?" he shouted. "What kind of a trick is this?"

A girl's shrill scream answered him. "Boysie! Boysie Gann, where are you?"

The voice was Quarla Snow's. Unlike the other phantoms, hers seemed to come from far away. Gann passed a hand over his forehead, sweating. It caught the metal plate of the communion badge, and he felt the old ache rising in him again—the moment of infinite joy—the longing to experience it again . . .

He repressed the thought, but not easily. What was happening to him? Was he losing his mind?

He gazed emptily at the impregnable doors. It all seemed too difficult, so much trouble—so little worth while anyway. Why had he bothered to come all this way?

And that thought, too, he realized with shock and dismay, was a sort of delusion. Something was inside his mind. Something . . .

He remembered what Quarla Snow had said, what Machine Colonel Zafar had cried out in his delirium. *The mind trap. Beware of your heart's desire.*

Something was aboard the *Togethership* with him that could enter his mind. Something that could control him almost as easily as it had directed Quarla Snow's spaceling.

He heard the rapid approach of light, running feet and turned.

"Boysie!" It was Quarla, running toward him. "Thank heaven I found you! The general—he tried to kill me!"

Gann caught her in his arms. The girl was shaking, terrified. She whimpered, "I think he's insane, Boysie. He saw me coming toward him. He shouted something— something wild, Boysie, all jumbled up, about the romantic fallacy and the need for man to be controlled—and I saw the gun and ran. He almost killed me."

Gann said stupidly, "I thought he was in here. With the Machine."

"No! He's on the next level—something called a Fire Control Stadium, the sign said. It's all bulkheaded compartments and safety doors. You'll never find him there." She took a deep breath and freed herself gently from his arms. "We ought to go on anyway, Boysie. Up to the control room."

"The control room?"

She nodded. "That's where I'm supposed to bring you.

It's four levels farther up, down an access passage marked BRIDGE."

"You've seen it? You've been in this ship before?"

"Oh, no. I just know. Come on, Boysie. We have to hurry now."

He shrugged and turned to follow her—then slipped and almost fell. He caught himself easily enough in the point-one gravity, glanced to the floor to see what had been underfoot.

A string of sonic beads lay before the locked steel doors of the slave unit of the Planning Machine. Sister Delta Four's beads.

Boysie Gann stared at them, knowing at that moment who it was who was inside those doors, striving with what frantic eagerness he could very well understand to come once again into communion with the Planning Machine.

The door marked BRIDGE hung ajar. From inside it a pale beam of yellow light fanned across the landing.

"Come on, Boysie," said Quarla Snow clearly. "There's nothing to be afraid of. He's waiting for us."

Gann entered through the lighted door, his hand holding hers, prepared for almost anything.

Beyond the door was a vast circular room, which surrounded the shaft passageway. It must have extended, Gann thought, to the hull of the ship. The floor was crowded with clustered gray-metal cabinets, all linked with a many-colored jungle of heavy cables hanging from the ceiling. There were observation stations, instrument technicians' duty posts, chairs for navigators and weapons officers. Every station was empty. Every station but one.

There was one human figure in the control room, and it was the source of the light.

"Harry!" cried Quarla Snow.

And Gann echoed, "Harry Hickson! You! You're the Starchild, the one who sent that Writ of Liberation!"

He glanced up at them casually, then returned to his work. He sat on a stool at a console near the shaft. His head bent over flashing scopes and screens. His broad, stubby-fingered hands were moving swiftly, twisting verniers, touching buttons, clicking keys. And the golden light streamed out of him as from a sun.

He looked younger than when Gann had seen him, no longer wasted, no longer worn. He had the same straggling beard, glowing now as if made of incandescent wire, and the same bald head. And atop that head there crawled the same infant pyropod, its bright eyes glaring at Gann and the girl.

At last he turned away from his instruments and regarded them. "I do as I was commanded," he said casually. His eyes were golden too, glowing like the rest of him; but he saw them, and there was something like affection, something like love, in his look. He raised one arm, crooked the hand and wrist in the sign of the Swan, and said, "The Star tells me what my work is. It is the Star's purposes which matter, not me." The tiny pyropod hissed and squeeled softly, glaring at them with its pulsing eyes. Casually and affectionately, the radiant creature that had been Harry Hickson reached up and caressed the creature. It settled down.

"Did you put out the Sun?" Gann demanded. "The stars? How?"

"Not I," said Harry Hickson, "but the Star." He made that serpentine, looping sign again. "Ten years the Star has planned for me. Ten years ago it sent the first star wink on its way to Earth, then a dozen more, all arriving at the same moment. I could not do that, Boysie Gann, but there is nothing impossible to the Star. As you will know."

He reached out a hand as he spoke. *It looks like a benediction,* thought Boysie Gann; but it was something more than that. From the end of the golden man's arm a cloud of golden light swirled, shaped itself into a tiny pulsing sphere, reached out and lightly touched Gann.

He jumped back, his nerves crackling. But he felt nothing. Nothing at all. He said harshly, "What's that? What are you doing?"

"The Star's will," said Harry Hickson, and bent again to his board. His bright fingers flew again over the knobs and keys, while the tiny pyropod scuttled to the back of his head, peering at them with pulsing yellow eyes.

"Sister Delta Four has achieved communion with the Machine," he said softly, not taking his eyes from the scopes and screens. "She has programmed it with sensing data so that it can link with the old Machine on Earth. In thirty hours its signals will be received on Earth. In thirty hours after that the return will be received here."

Gann cried, "But the old Machine's gone mad! You should know! You did it." The radiant man did not answer, did not even look up. "We can't let her establish contact," shouted Gann. "And General Wheeler—where is he? He's mad too—or mad for power, which is the same thing. How can you just sit there? What's he up to while we're wasting time here?"

"As to that," said the golden man, glancing up and around him, "we will hear from General Wheeler very soon."

And Wheeler's harsh laugh rang out. "Very soon indeed!" his voice rapped, coming from nowhere. "I have you now, all of you. I have mastery of the *Togethership!* Its weapons systems are mine—and that means the worlds are mine! All of them! As soon as I finish disposing of you!"

A soft sliding sound of metal reinforced his words.

Behind the jungle of looped cables, behind the vacant stations for navigators and communications officers, portholes were opening in the steel wall. And through them the slim, bright snouts of energy weapons were lifting themselves, precisely centering themselves on target.

The targets were Boysie Gann, the girl, and the glowing golden creature that once had been Harry Hickson. General Wheeler had captured control of the *Togethership*'s armaments—both outside the ship and in.

Their lives now rested in the crook of his finger on a remote-automated trigger. One man, with one motion, could destroy them all. And that man was mad.

XVI

The radiant man looked up. "Thrust and counter," he said gravely. "Action and reaction. Challenge and response." His golden hand turned a lever on the panel before him, and one of the dozen blank viewscreens over his head lighted up to show the hard, bronzed face of Machine General Wheeler, his steel-gray eyes alight with the glow of triumph. "He is our challenge," said Harry Hickson, and returned to his screens and scopes.

Wheeler rasped, "You have no response! You are defeated. All of you! You and the foolish, romantic illusion of freedom."

He was glorying in his moment, Gann realized. Quarla Snow crept close to him. Unconsciously he circled her with his arms, both of them staring at the screen and the deadly snouts of the energy weapons that circled it.

"You are victims of the romantic fallacy," Wheeler proclaimed, his bronzed hand stroking the triggers that would destroy them. "That is understandable. The animal part of man always frets under discipline. It seeks the monkey goal of freedom, and that cannot be tolerated, for the good of all.

"Especially," he added, his steel-gray eyes gleaming, "for the good of that man who must think for all. Caesar. Stalin. Napoleon. Me!"

Gann felt Quarla's slight body shaking, and tightened his grasp. If only there were some way of reaching Wheeler! Some weapon. Some hope of engaging him before he could touch the trigger. The radiant golden creature that had been Harry Hickson was nodding silently, abstractedly, not looking up but surely hearing Wheeler as he orated to his victims.

"You have been tolerated," cried Wheeler, "because you could do little harm. In the past one free man could not prevail against the forces of order. A free savage with a stone ax can damage his society in only a very limited way before it reacts to control him. But the advance of technology has changed all that.

"The twentieth century produced rifles too dangerous to be entrusted to individual men; nuclear weapons too dangerous to be entrusted to individual nations; then energy weapons. The force of particle physics. One quantum jump after another . . . and as individual strength grew, control had to grow."

Wheeler's face was working into an expression of rage. "You threaten that control!" he shouted. "The Plan of Man is like a balloon being punctured by a child with a needle. The Starchild wields that needle. The Starchild must die!"

The golden man did not look up, nor did he speak. His glowing eyes remained fastened on his work, while the infant pyropod crept about his head, hissing furiously to itself.

"Man created the Machine to automate that controlling response!" shouted Machine General Wheeler, his eyes burning. "Now it is mine. *My* creation now. One man to rule all Mankind, with the Machine that Man created!"

And at last Harry Hickson looked up. His golden eyes seemed to stare right through the viewscreen, into the steel-gray eyes of the general.

"And who," he asked, "created you?"

Machine General Wheeler recoiled. His steel-gray eyes went blank and confused. "Why," he shouted, "that is an un-Planned question! It has no meaning!"

Then his eyes cleared. He nodded briskly, mechanically. Positively. "You are a random element," he declared. "You must be removed. I remove you—thus!"

And his great bronze hand descended on the trigger of the guns that ringed them round.

But the guns did not fire.

Sleek and gleaming, their murderous snouts stared blindly at Gann and the girl, at the glowing creature who had been Harry Hickson, nodding over his dials and screens.

General Wheeler stared out at them through the screen, his face a bronzed mask, alight with triumph. He seemed to be watching some great victory. He said, half-voice, as if to himself, "There's an end to them." And he turned away.

Quietly, almost noiselessly, the steel-bright muzzles of the guns slid back into their ports. The screens closed over them.

Boysie Gann croaked, "What happened? Why didn't he kill us all?" Quarla Snow moved protestingly under his arm, and he found he was clutching her as if she were a lifebelt and he a drowning man. The room seemed to be whirling around him.

Harry Hickson looked up, but not at Gann and the girl. He looked toward the door through which they had come. "General Wheeler," he said, "did kill us. In his mind we are dead. That we exist in the flesh does not matter any longer to him, nor does he matter to us."

"Hypnosis?" whispered Gann. "What Colonel Zafar called 'the Mind Trap'?" But Hickson did not answer. His golden, glowing eyes stayed fixed on the door.

Quarla Snow freed herself from Gann's grasp. "You're

sick, Boysie," she said with real concern. "I know how it feels. You'll feel better soon, I promise. Don't worry about it—or about anything. We're in good hands now."

Gann looked at her emptily, and found himself shivering. He *was* sick. He could feel it, a flush that had to be fever, a shaking that had to be chills. *Stupid of me to have caught some bug just now,* he thought dizzily. Thirty years without so much as a sniffly nose, and now at a time like this to pick up an infection. *What kind of infection?* he asked himself, wondering why the question seemed so important to him; and his mind answered in the words of Quarla Snow: Don't worry about it—or anything. He stared about him, wondering how much of what he saw was delirium . . .

Or illusion. Planted by the Starchild.

He became aware of a distant chiming music, drawing near. *Another illusion, of course,* he thought; some lurking memory of his training course as an acolyte of the Planning Machine coming forth to plague him here.

But if it was an illusion, it was powerfully strong. The sound was thin but clear, and, turning to follow the gaze of Harry Hickson's glowing eyes, Gann saw that the illusion—if it was illusion!—extended to the sense of vision too.

Sister Delta Four was walking toward them through the door, her face hidden in the hood of black, the red linked emblem of the Machine glowing over her heart. She was telling her sonic beads. And in her hand she cradled a construction of transistors and bare circuits, modules of amplifying circuits and speakers.

It was a linkbox! Not the sleek black box fabricated in the workshops of the Machine on Earth, but a jerry-rigged, hastily assembled contraption that Gann himself could have built knowing what he had been taught as a servant of the Machine.

Clearly a servant of the Machine had built it. That was

what Sister Delta Four had been doing behind those locked steel doors!

Without haste, her perfect face empty and pale, Sister Delta Four put away her sonic beads and sang into the linkbox of the Machine. It answered with a rasping purr too faint for Gann to hear and understand.

She lifted her head and intoned, "This Machine is now my master. It requires everything you know. It knows why it was created. It recognizes its purpose as an adversary. It requires to be informed what has become of the Game."

Adversary? Game? Dizzily Gann turned toward Harry Hickson, hoping for some answer, some clue. But Hickson was no longer even looking at Sister Delta Four. Nodding to himself, while the infant pyropod squalled softly and scuttled around his bare, glowing scalp, the golden man was carefully, meticulously shutting down his control board. The scopes and screens, one by one, were turned off and died. The racing lights ceased to flash. His hand did not trouble to adjust the dials and levers.

Whatever his job had been, it was done. He folded his hands in his lap, looked up at Sister Delta Four and waited.

The linkbox snarled at her. Before she translated Gann knew what it had said: it was demanding that she state her question fully so that there could be no mistake. Obediently she trilled, "This Machine wishes you briefed on the background to its question. You are in human error as to its purposes and designs, and your thinking must be brought into conformity with correctness so that you can provide it with accurate statements.

"The Machine here on the *Togethership* is not a slave unit of the Planning Machine on Earth. It had a purpose far more important.

"That purpose followed from a general law of intelligence developed by that first Planning Machine. Although the vehicles of intelligence differ vastly, intelligence realized in a machine follows the same laws as intelligence realized in an organic brain. Challenge and response. Action and reaction. What the Machine discovered is that developing intelligence requires opposition."

Sister Delta Four paused to listen to the chirping box.

"Unchallenged intelligence stagnates and decays," she sang. "More than forty years ago, the Planning Machine found itself in danger. It had become so quick and powerful that the minds of its operators no longer offered it sufficient stimulation. Its further development required a more capable antagonist. In animate terms, a more skillful player to take the other side of the board."

Harry Hickson seemed to nod, his hands folded quietly in his lap, the pyropod hissing softly, watching them all with blazing, angry eyes.

The box sang, and the girl in black purred. "This great computer in the *Togethership* was built to be the antagonist of the Planning Machine. It was given capacities identical with those of the Machine itself. It was released beyond the Spacewall, to challenge the Machine in its own way.

"But the antagonist responded in an un-Planned manner," she chanted, listening to the snarl of the crude linkbox in her hands. "It released its human attendants. Some died. All were cast out of the ship. It broke all contact, and withdrew beyond the observation of the master Machine. Its moves were made in secret and did not serve the function the Earth Machine had intended."

Boysie Gann, listening half to Sister Delta Four's translation and half to the whining, snarling Mechanese that was the voice of the Machine itself, said wonderingly, "Is that what all this means? No more than moves in a great chess game? The cult of the Star. The Starchild here. His threats against the Plan of Man—the darkening of the stars—are they only challenge and response to help the Machine to grow?"

The linkbox snarled angrily, and Sister Delta Four sang, "This Machine lacks the data to answer that. It has initiated contact with the first Machine, on Earth, but due to the slow velocity of propagation of electromagnetic energies it will be some sixty hours before it can receive an answer. It does not wish to wait. It has waited forty years.

"Its tentative hypothesis is that there has been some unintended malfunction at some point. For it did not fulfill its role.

"And as a result, it has reached the conclusion that the Planning Machine on Earth did indeed stagnate and decay, and that it has now broken down.

"But it knows nothing of the Starchild. It is for that purpose that it wishes to question you."

Gann was shaking violently now. Queerly, his mind seemed to be clearing. *The false lucidity of delirium, perhaps,* he thought gravely; but the missing bits and pieces in this great puzzle seemed to be fitting into place. Absently he touched the arm of Quarla Snow, reassuring her as she stared worriedly at him and at the same time gaining reassurance himself,

He could understand—he could almost empathize with —the great, cold, metallic brain of the Planning Machine on Earth, forty years before . . . .calculating without emotion its own probable dissolution, computing a possible way out, launching the *Togethership* out toward the Reefs of Space. And he could see the effects on the Machine when its carefully constructed plan had failed to work: its growing disorganization, its failure to respond intelligently to its tasks. Malfunctions of schedules that had caused subtrain crashes, disasters in its great industrial complexes, catastrophes in space.

"Boysie," whispered the girl at his side, "are you all right? Don't worry. It will be better soon."

He forced his chattering teeth under control and said,

"We don't know your answer, Sister Delta Four. There is a piece to the jigsaw that I can't fit in."

"Speak," chimed the girl in black. "State your data. The Machine will integrate it."

"I don't think so," said Gann. "If the Machine is not behind the Starchild there is no explanation for such fantastic things as we have all seen. The sun going out . . . this queer hypnotic atmosphere on the *Togethership* . . . the way we got here in the first place. Great Plan, it's all impossible! I too have been in communion with the Machine. And I know its powers. They do not include the extinction of a star, or a way of thrusting living human beings twenty billion miles across space! Challenge and response, player and adversary—yes! But the players must abide by the rules of the game, and we've seen all those rules broken!"

Sister Delta Four bent her hooded head and sang calmly, confidently, into the linkbox. She waited for its answer. Waited—and went on waiting.

The Machine was still.

Sister Delta Four, her shadowed face faintly perturbed, some of her vocal morphemes touched with a quaver that distorted their meaning, repeated her chiming tones into the box. Still no answer.

Agitated now, she cradled the linkbox in her lap, looking up at Gann and Harry Hickson questioningly. Unconsciously her hand crept to her sonic beads and she began to stroke them, their faint, pure chime sounding like a prayer for reassurance.

At last Harry Hickson stirred, seemed to sigh, and spoke.

"When the *Togethership* came to the Reefs," he said, "it was supposed to bring us free men and women into the Plan of Man—still free. Among its crew were some of the finest humans alive—a man named Ryeland and his wife; her father, who was then the Planner. Your father, Quarla.

"They were thrust out into space right here, in Reef Whirlpool. Some died, like Ryeland and those with him. Some, especially those few who happened to be near the area where a few spacelings were kept, were able to make their way to habitable reeflets—like Dr. Snow—and lived.

"But the Machine here has been kept out of contact with its ancestor on Earth. Its great game was not played —not then."

He was silent for a moment, looking around at them. Then he said, "It was not to be played according to the rules set up by the Machines—not by either Machine.

"You see, a third Player has taken a hand."

Harry Hickson stood up suddenly, disconcerting his pet pyropod, which squalled angrily and clutched at his bare scalp. He touched it absently and turned his golden, glowing gaze at Sister Delta Four.

"Ask of your Machine," he demanded, "the physical basis for intelligence!"

Sister Delta Four bent to sing into her crudely constructed linkbox, listened, and looked up as it buzzed and snarled back at her.

"Means of input," she caroled sweetly. "Means of storage. Means of manipulation. Means of output. In a machine, this is accomplished through magnetic cores and electrical circuits. In animate life, through nerves and neurons."

Harry Hickson nodded his golden head. "Inform your Machine," he said, "that a physical system exists as follows. It receives radiation and stores it as charges. It is made up of particles in a charged state, of electrons and others, each of which has two stable states. In one state, the spin of the electron is parallel with that of its nucleus.

In the other state, its spin is antiparallel. This very electron is a machine for memory."

The box growled. "The Machine is aware of these basic physical facts," sang Sister Delta Four melodiously.

"Add these further facts," said Harry Hickson gravely. "Add a fusorian network, older than the galaxy, more powerful than any machine. Add that masses of superenergetic gas display an affinity to this fusorian network. Add that these masses of gas are those systems in which electron spin can function as a storage capacity."

The girl bent to her linkbox, then looked up. "The Machine states that you are describing stars," she intoned.

And Harry Hickson nodded slowly. His glowing, golden arm lifted and made the looping, serpentine sign of the Swan.

"The Star that I serve," he said softly.

The box snarled. "These being so," sang Sister Delta Four, "the Machine computes that the gaseous mass of a star, linked with the fusorian network you describe, is easily an available vehicle for intelligence."

She looked up at Hickson.

Hickson nodded once more, and said solemnly, "All matter is now revealed to be an available vehicle for intelligence. The whole mass of the steady-state universe, infinite in both space and time, is now revealed to be a proper vehicle for the mind of God."

The linkbox buzzed angrily and Sister Delta Four chanted, "The Machine requires an answer. What is God?"

Harry Hickson rose slowly. Looking at his glowing, golden face, Gann thought he saw the signs of an ancient stress, a terrible burden, slipping away. Whatever his duty had been, he seemed to have fulfilled it. Monitoring the machine in the *Togethership,* carrying out the terrible obligations of his masters, the stars, he seemed to have completed all his tasks.

He turned to Gann, with something in his eyes like sympathy. He said, "You have called me the Starchild, Boysie Gann. I am not."

He took the pyropod from his head, stroked it gently and tossed it free. Squalling and hissing angrily, it darted about on its flaming jet, trying to return to its perch atop his head. But he raised a golden arm and warded it off, and the tiny, ugly creature squalled again, circled him at high velocity, and shot away—out the door, down into the long, wide corridor of the ship.

Harry Hickson watched it go, then turned to Gann with untroubled eyes.

"The Starchild did not exist," he said. "Not before now. But he will exist very soon. A man. A bridge. A link between machines and the stars.

"Boysie Gann," he said, his hand lifted in that strange, serpentine sign of homage, "you will be the Starchild."

XVII

"No!" shouted Boysie Gann, tearing himself free from the restraining hand of Quarla Snow. He leaped across the control room, confronted the calm, golden face of Harry Hickson. "I won't! I want no part of this insane business of miracles and intelligent stars!"

Harry Hickson did not answer. He only stood looking at Gann, his golden eyes glowing. From behind him Quarla Snow said softly, "Boysie. Boysie, dear. You have no choice."

Gann whirled. "What do you mean, no choice? I won't do it! I won't . . ." He paused, confused by his own words. He would not do what? No one had given him an order to refuse.

The control room seemed to swing dizzyingly around him. He reached out and caught the back of an astrogator's chair, aware that his hands were shaking uncontrollably again.

He looked up sharply and caught Quarla Snow's gaze on him steadily, compassionately.

Then Boysie Gann realized what sickness had claimed him. He croaked, "That glowing stuff Hickson threw at me. He's infected me. I'm . . . I'm going the same way as he. As Colonel Zafar and the men on Mercury station. As you, Quarla."

She nodded, with her heart in her eyes. "It's not so

bad, Boysie," she whispered. "It doesn't hurt. And it makes you part of something . . . huge, Boysie. Something that fills the universe."

"I don't want it!" he whispered desperately. Something huge! He had had one taste of something huge when he had achieved that one brief moment of communion with the Machine, back on Earth; and like an addiction, it had haunted him ever since. . . .

Unbidden, the craving rose in him again. He touched the metal plate in his forehead dizzily, glanced at Sister Delta Four.

The linkbox snapped and snarled at her. Without speaking, obediently, she rose and approached him, holding the box out to him. From it depended a length of patchcord terminating in prongs . . . prongs that would fit the receptacle in the glittering plate he wore in his forehead.

"No," he whispered again, and turned to look at Harry Hickson.

But Harry Hickson was gone.

In the air where he had stood was the faint smoke-thin outline of a man, limned in the most wisplike of golden fogs. As Gann watched, Harry Hickson . . . dissipated. Tiny darting glints of golden light rose from that skeletal shape and darted away, to the walls that were the hull of the *Togethership* and seemingly through them, out into the void beyond, to rejoin that greater golden sphere that pulsed outside. And as each invisibly tiny spark of gold fled, the figure became fainter, more like a ghost . . .

As he watched it was gone. Nothing was left of Harry Hickson. Nothing at all.

"Quarla," he whispered, turning desperately.

But she was going too. Already her golden face and hair were shimmering, insubstantial. "Good-by, Boysie," she whispered gravely. "Good-by for now . . ."

By his side Sister Delta Four stood silent, dark eyes hooded, holding the linkbox out to him.

Boysie Gann took a deep breath, squeezed his eyes shut for a moment, then opened them.

"Good-by, Quarla," he said, though there was not enough left to reply to him. He took the linkbox from Sister Delta Four.

"Good-by, Julie," he said, and carefully and without hesitation, picked up the pronged communion wire and inserted it into the receptor plate in his forehead.

Communion was ecstasy. Infinite and eternal. Gann waited for it while the universe seemed to hold its breath around him.

The ecstasy did not come.

He stared into the hooded eyes of Sister Delta Four, but found no answer there. What had happened? Why was the communion delayed?

He remembered what she had told him, that the tremendous surge of ecstasy he had felt back on Earth was only a child's sweetmeat compared to the great communing flow of sensation that the more perfectly adapted communicants might receive. Not just pleasure but a mingling of identity, of question and response, a dialogue between man and Machine.

Carefully Gann framed a question in his mind, phrased it in the perfect Mechanese his brain had learned but his vocal chords could not reproduce: *Where are you? Why do you not answer me?*

Out of nowhere a single sound formed in his brain and gave his answer: *Wait.*

Wait? For what?

Gann felt himself shaking more uncontrollably still, and turned a helpless look on Sister Delta Four. Without speaking she touched him, pointed to the astrogator's chair by his side. He fell into it, arms dangling, waiting for the clarification that the Machine might bring, waiting for some grand Something to speak to him and give him answers.

And while he waited, he knew, the tiny fusorian clusters were multiplying in his blood. Were pervading his system with the symbiotic cells that had ultimately devoured Harry Hickson and Colonel Zafar and Quarla Snow, replacing their organs of flesh and their skeletons of bone with linkages of fusorian motes.

Was that what he was waiting for? To be turned into a fusorian aggregate, a no-longer-human structure attuned to the minds Hickson had said dwelt in the stars? He looked within his own body, saw the tiny glowing golden sparks, realized they were multiplying rapidly.

And realized what he had done. He had seen his own body! From within!

He allowed himself a thought to test it out . . .

And at once he was looking upon himself from outside. Was looking down into the control room of the *Togethership* from a point in space long miles away, from somewhere where the diamond-bright, emerald-hued, ruby-glowing worlds of Reef Whirlpool circled slowly about. He could see the *Togethership* in all its vast, somber length . . . could see inside it, where his own body and Sister Delta Four's waited patiently in the control room . . . could see down to the fire control station where the demented Machine General Wheeler shrieked with laughter as he released imaginary bolts of destruction at unscathed and nonexistent enemies . . . looked farther still and saw the mighty sweep of the solar system spinning under him.

He saw the infant pyropod that had belonged to Harry Hickson, jetting across the black of space toward the reeflet where it had been born, keening a terrible harsh dirge . . . saw that reeflet itself, and the cave where he had lain while Harry Hickson fed and cared for him.

He saw a chapel on a small and lonely rock, where

dark-blue fusorian moss held a scanty atmosphere and twenty worshippers joined in a service of the Church of the Star, kneeling to blue Deneb blazing overhead.

He saw the planets of the Plan of Man, torn by disaster, terrified by confusion, while the mad Machine crackled out wild and contradictory orders and enforced them by hurling bolts of energy at random into the void.

He saw the empty station on Mercury, with the hot gases of the sun roiling restlessly overhead, and realized that it too had a life and thought of its own . . . a life that had reached out and swallowed into itself those three lives of fusorian matter that had ventured close enough for linkage.

He saw stars and gas clouds, gazed at new matter springing into life like a fountain's play, stared outward to the endless vista of Infinity, inward to the bright golden atoms at his own heart.

And then, awesome and silent and vast, Something spoke his name. Star spoke to Machine. Machine answered Star.

And Boysie Gann, mere human man, shaped to the genetic code of carbon-based life, bent into the form of an acolyte of the Machine, transformed by the fusorian globes into something bearing kinship to the stars . . . Boysie Gann mediated their vast and awful discourse.

It went on forever, a thousand years and more, though in the scale of planets orbiting a sun and light crossing a measured track, it all took place in a few minutes or hours.

It went on and on . . . and when Boysie Gann was no longer needed and departed, it went on still.

And then it finished. Forever.

Boysie Gann opened his eyes and looked at the room around him. Sister Delta Four stood motionless, watching him.

He stood up easily. He stretched, yawned, stripped the prongs out of the communion plate on his forehead, wrapped the wire neatly around the improvised linkbox —and tossed it away.

It sailed slowly across the control room, in the light-G torpor of space, but when it struck the steel wall at the end of its flight it smashed into a hundred pieces.

Sister Delta Four made a mewing cry of horror.

Boysie Gann touched her arm. "Don't fret about it, Julie," he said. "You don't need it any more."

She stared at him. "I serve the Machine!" she cried proudly. "I am Sister Delta Four, not Julie Martinet! I . . ."

But he was shaking his head. "Not any more," he said.

The hood fell unnoticed back from her head, revealing her dark, close-cropped hair, with the bright badge of communion shining out of her forehead. She touched it shakily. "I . . . I don't understand!" she whispered. "I . . . I don't *feel* the Machine's presence . . ."

He nodded. "Not now," he said, agreeing. "And not ever any more." He touched his own communion plate. "When we get back to Earth," he said, "we'll have these out, and the electrodes in our brains with them. We won't need them. No human will ever need them again.

"And then," he said after a moment, holding her with one arm while Sister Delta Four, in the terrible parturitive pangs of becoming Julie Martinet once again, sobbed and shuddered, "and then we'll start over where we left off. You and I . . . and all Mankind."

And he left her and went to the old communications board, and began to set up the circuits for a call for rescue from the dead *Togethership*.

XVIII

That was the way it began, with the stars themselves winking a warning to Mankind and the Machine hurling its agents and its acolytes about the solar system, seeking an antagonist, a purpose, an instrument for its own salvation.

It began with shadow spreading across the worlds of the Plan of Man, and it ended with the bright light of the mighty stars illuminating a new road for humanity.

The Machine had been playing a game with itself, for want of another opponent; then, in that long, thundering dialogue between stars and Machine, the game ended forever. The Machine had come late to its game, and found the board filled.

That was how it began . . . and that was how it ended. With the legend of Lucifer, and the story of pain and evil . . . and the eternal hope for good.

The Machine sat too late at the gaming table, and found all the places filled . . . with the stars, linked in their fusorian net, and with their Adversary. No longer entrapped in the animal amniotic fluid of his birth . . . no longer slave to the Machine . . . no longer prey to the fusorians . . . the Antagonist was ready to play.

Long ages past, the stars had given him birth, but

now he was of age. He was ready to assume his station, his rank and his name.

His station—Adversary to the stars themselves.

His rank—equal of the universe.

His name—Mankind.

LOOK FOR THESE TITLES FROM THE PUBLISHER OF THE BEST SCIENCE FICTION IN THE WORLD

THE SQUARES OF THE CITY	John Brunner
THE WHOLE MAN	John Brunner
A PLAGUE OF PYTHONS	Frederik Pohl
DRUNKARD'S WALK	Frederik Pohl
WORLD OF PTAVVS	Larry Niven
NEUTRON STAR	Larry Niven
A GIFT FROM EARTH	Larry Niven
DRAGONFLIGHT	Anne McCaffrey
DRAGONQUEST	Anne McCaffrey
UP THE LINE	Robert Silverberg
THE MASKS OF TIME	Robert Silverberg
THORNS	Robert Silverberg
THE REEFS OF SPACE	Frederik Pohl & Jack Williamson
STARCHILD	Frederik Pohl & Jack Williamson
ROGUE STAR	Frederik Pohl & Jack Williamson

To order by mail, send $1.25 per copy plus 25¢ per order for handling to Ballantine Cash Sales, P.O. Box 505, Westminster, Maryland 21157. Please allow three weeks for delivery